The Day
AFTER LIFE

'The Way Station' Part III

By Minister Larry Montgomery, Sr.
Author of U.S. Marshal Harry Bailey
and the Parables of Life Series

The DAY AFTER LIFE

Author Minister Larry Montgomery, Sr.

montgomerybusiness@hotmail.com

THE DAY AFTER LIFE

ISBN: 978-0-9861290-8-7

Published by Emerging Business Group, Inc.

Baldwin, New York.

THE DAY AFTER LIFE

Dedicated to my wife Joyous and
my children for their love and support

THE DAY AFTER LIFE

ABOUT THIS BOOK

This the final installment in the Christian Fiction series: Way Station Part I, Beyond the Way Station Part II—To Hell for the Holidays, The Way Station Part III -- The Day After Life.

If your goal is to get to Heaven then here is one interpretation from the book designed to provide Basic Instruction Before Leaving Earth; better known as the BIBLE, of what will happen the Day After Life.

Life is like a basketball game or any other team sport. The coach (God) sends you in to help win the game. The goal of Life is to win as interpreted by the one who created the game in the first place (God). So with that picture in your mind let me complete my explanation of the game of Life; the told you to go in and win the game. That is the same thing he told all of the other players in the locker room. The Coach gave everyone their individual assignments; they practiced their assignments within the context of the play's the Coach designed. The Coach told every one about the opponent's strengths, strategies, even the individual players the opponent will be using during the game.

You on the other hand seemingly understood every thing the Coach has explained, you were given the play book (Bible) and told to study it in preparation for the is big game. You've seen the film clips of some of your opponent's team mates (Nightmares and real life meanies) and you've practiced how to defend them, or keep them from scoring.

Now you walk on the court, we are talking about basketball

THE DAY AFTER LIFE

here, and all you can remember is score as many points as possible and you will obtain the goal that the coach sent you in to do. As the game gets going the only things that cross your mind are scoring, then assisting and then defending. Occasionally someone calls for a particular play to be run and you suddenly find yourself confused or distracted not knowing whether to pass the ball to the open man or to stick to the designated play and hit the man at the spot he is supposed to be at.

Now the final buzzer has rung and the game is over you are in the locker room and the Coach is going over your performance during the game that lead to the final score. How do you think this conversation is going to go when the Coach will not tell you the final score before the conversation begins?

The Day After Life is that moment when the game is over and the score board is being tallied but the Coach is questioning your performance on the court. Not knowing whether your team won or not or if you will receive the MVP or be kicked off the team you face the litany of opened questions from the press, the fans, the Coach and the Teams Owner while awaiting the ultimate decision. Will your contract be approved?

Follow four team players through this life's final inquiry, the one that determines where their soul's next final resting place will be the Day After Life.

THE DAY AFTER LIFE

ABOUT THE AUTHOR:

Minister Larry Montgomery, Sr., is a retired Banker currently publishing the only online weekly African-American community newspaper on Long Island. Minister Montgomery, Sr. holds a MBA from Hofstra University, Hempstead, New York where he grew up, married and raised three loving children.

Minister Montgomery is a member of Glory Temple Ministries, Inc., Massapequa, New York where under the Pastorship of Senior Pastor Apostle Bishop Ronnie Deadwyler and Executive Pastor Apostle Bishop Dr. Karen Deadwyler, who in obedience to the Father, planted the seed of "Scribe" on Minister Montgomery's heart. To that end, Minister Montgomery committed to penning twelve of the Lord's parables under the cover of the life and times of a fictional character named U.S. Marshal Harry Bailey, entitled: U.S. Marshal Harry Bailey and the Parables of Life series.

That was twelve books ago. Since then Minister Montgomery has written four additional fictional short stories entitled; "The Game of Your Life" and "The Way Station", "2-1-1 Emergency", "Clinical Trials" and a Special Anniversary Edition of U.S. Marshal Harry Bailey entitled: "The CORPORATE KILLINGS" and the Case of the "Deadly Mailman".

He hopes that you enjoy reading this effort as much as you did or will do when reading any of his previous efforts.

Thank you for considering this work and please feel free to pass it on. We hope you find a few moments of relaxation when reading this book and that you look forward to reading our most recent efforts entitled "Criminal Mastermind" and "Beyond the Way Station Part II-To Hell for the Holidays" and this one "The Way Station Part III-'The Day After Life'".

May God continue to Bless You and Yours!

THE DAY AFTER LIFE

TABLE OF CONTENTS

LIST OF OTHER BOOK PROJECTS CAN BE FOUND ON PAGE 166

THE DAY AFTER LIFE

CHAPTER 1

INTRODUCTION

This is the final installment in the "Way Station" trilogy which has provided some insightful insight into the hereafter, from a Christian point of view. The first effort, the Way Station present the idea that death can happen at anytime, and that means that a death in your life doesn't have to mean your life is over; it could merely the life you knew has ended. That God has given you a second chance at life not to get it right but to accomplish what it is he had planned for you to do.

In that book we followed six (6) fictional characters to a place where they can make a choice as to where their souls will go next. They determine this on their own in some cases and in other cases it is determined for them.

Our second effort in this three book series is entitled; "Beyond the Way Station, Part II – To Hell for the Holidays. That book focuses on now that you have died what from a preliminary perspective where will your soul go; to Heaven or to Hell?

That book focused on the results of the choices four (4) fictional characters make when their souls are finally required. In other words this book differs from volume 1 in that the characters are prescreened for their next transition in life after being processed at the Way Station. At the Way Station they were given the opportunity to make to choose however now that they have received that bit of grace, the next realm in life requires that someone else offers input towards their next choice of where their soul will transition to.

Volume II set's the stage for volume III, entitled: "The Day After Life". Here the soul's of four (4) fictional characters have transitioned through the "Way Station" and made a choice based on the motives from their past and they have come "Beyond the Way Station..." to find themselves no longer in control but having to defend the motives behind the choices they made: to the final stage. The point of no return, they are all dead and their souls are being required by God and it is judgment time.

In this book these fictional characters face their final judgment on the Day After their Life has ended.

This book presents the final trial with God the judge, the devil as prosecutor and the angel of God as the defense attorney.

Before you can sit in the court gallery you must fully understand certain Godly principal's, or laws:

THREE SPIRITUAL LAWS

We are all governed by laws. Right now somewhere on earth there is a political battle going on over whom will be the law maker. The liberal's want more laws and more regulations to protect and take care of people. The conservative's want fewer laws, believing less is better. Whichever party is elected they will have the power to write new laws or decommission old ones. The President, Prime Minister, King or Queen whether

THE DAY AFTER LIFE

liberal or conservative, will sign those laws into effect that he (or she) and his or hers party agrees with.

When a soul faces its final judgment God refers to His own laws to judge it by. And in His wisdom, to show that He is a good God and worthy of all Glory and Praise He has written those laws down and given them to each of us in what many would call the Book of Laws. Or in other words Basic Instruction Before Leaving Earth, the BIBLE.

As a back drop let's start here, at a place during Old Testament times when people lived under the 'Law."

During that time judgment was based on the "Levitical Laws". Those were the laws that God gave Moses to pass on to His people. They included the "Ten Commandments". When you think of these laws – you can simply substitute the word (God's) 'will' instead of (God's) 'law' and it may make it easier to understand. Instead of the "Ten Commandments" think of it as "10 things that are God's will". Now the Levitical law can all be summed up with one key point: Paul writes.

"The entire law is summed up in a single command: "Love your neighbor as yourself." [Lev. 19:18] (Galatians 5:14). "Love does no harm to its neighbor. Therefore love is the fulfillment of the law." Romans 13:10.

So, basically the Levitical law had to do with God's will. If you willfully go against God's will, you are in rebellion and will suffer the consequence of separation from God and His blessing. But, if you love God and express that love to God through obedience

THE DAY AFTER LIFE

to His known will in your life, that love covers a multitude of imperfections. Jesus paid for our sins with the shedding of His blood - so keeping the law doesn't justify us; but having a desire to do God's will and walking in obedience because of our love for Him, fulfills the law.

With that said; to understand the story that is about to be unfolded you need to accept some basic principals: Three laws that affect us every day. They are not legislative laws or scientific physical laws or even the Levitical law. They are spiritual laws and they affect us every day as much as any of these other laws do. Our lives are changed because of these laws. If we keep them – we are blessed. If we violate them; if we break them – we suffer the consequences.

The first law is the "Law of Life and death". The law of life and death is important because keeping this law brings life – and breaking this law brings death. The Bible says, "For the wages of sin is death, but the gift of God is eternal life in Christ Jesus our Lord." Romans 6:23.

Usually when we talk about this verse we are talking about the final consequence – which is eternal death or eternal life. The wages of sin – or the result of sinning is eternal death. We call that hell and it is eternal separation from God and all that is good. It has been described by Jesus as a lake of fire and a place where the worms never die and a place of absolute darkness and a place of total isolation –being all alone- for all eternity. That is the ultimate result of living a sinful life and not believing in God or his salvation.

THE DAY AFTER LIFE

But there is a more immediate consequence to rebelling against God's will. It is immediate death – or immediate separation from God and His blessing. It is not total, because as long as we are alive we are under God's prevenient grace. In other words, even the most wicked can enjoy some of God's goodness. They experience pleasure and happiness and satisfaction – sometimes even in a perverted way. They may get pleasure out of doing evil. But when we sin, there is an immediate separation from God and His blessing. God can not bless the wicked. You may experience some of God prevenient grace – but you are separated from His best blessings when you rebel and knowingly go against His will.

The bible says: "But your iniquities have separated you from your God; your sins have hidden his face from you, so that he will not hear." Isaiah 59:2.

"If I had cherished sin in my heart, the Lord would not have listened." Psalm 66:18. One way that sin separates us from God is that it hinders our prayer life. God does not listen to the person who is rebelling against Him. Someone said that the only prayer God hears from the rebellious is a prayer of repentance. That can be best understood if you imagine a child refusing to obey her mother and demanding something she wants at the same time. Do you think she would get it? Answer: Her request would not be heard until that attitude of rebellion has changed.

Another way we are separated from God's goodness when we rebel is that we are separated from His protection. Even the devil knows that. The Bible says, "Does Job fear God for

THE DAY AFTER LIFE

nothing?" Satan replied. "Have you not put a hedge around him and his household and everything he has? You have blessed the work of his hands, so that his flocks and herds are spread throughout the land." Job 1: 9-10.

Be mindful of the two-fold blessing in this Scripture? There is a hedge of protection around the righteous person and God also blesses the work of His hands.

In the "law of Life and Death" we experience immediate separation from God when we break this law and we experience some immediate 'life' when we obey this law. This law affects us every day. Every day, if you are living within that love relationship with the Lord, blessings come your way. You may even take them for granted. If you don't walk in love with the Lord, your prayers are hindered, you lose His protection and are under a curse. The next law goes into this a little more.

The second spiritual law is the law of the increase. Sometimes it is called the 'law of the tithe". God says, "Will a mere mortal rob God? Yet you rob me. "But you ask, 'How are we robbing you?' "In tithes and offerings. You are under a curse... because you are robbing me. Bring the whole tithe into the storehouse, that there may be food in my house. Test me in this," says the LORD Almighty, "and see if I will not throw open the floodgates of heaven and pour out so much blessing that there will not be room enough to store it. I will prevent pests from devouring your crops, and the vines in your fields will not drop their fruit before it is ripe," says the LORD Almighty." Malachi 3:8-11.

Notice that God blesses the work of our hands? Job was blessed

THE DAY AFTER LIFE

financially because of His obedience. In this Scripture God clearly promises a financial blessing when we walk in obedience. A loving relationship with God pays off- literally. Notice also that God blesses us when we walk in obedience and hinders us when we don't. David said, "You rebuke and discipline men for their sin; you consume their wealth like a moth— each man is but a breath. Selah" Psalm 39:11.

This is what the LORD Almighty says: "Give careful thought to your ways. You have planted much, but have harvested little. You eat, but never have enough. You drink, but never have your fill. You put on clothes, but are not warm. You earn wages, only to put them in a purse with holes in it." Haggai 1:5-6. "You expected much, but see, it turned out to be little. What you brought home, I blew away. Why?" declares the LORD Almighty. "Because of my house, which remains a ruin, while each of you is busy with his own house. Therefore, because of you the heavens have withheld their dew and the earth its crops. I called for a drought on the fields and the mountains, on the grain, the new wine, the olive oil and everything else the ground produces, on people and livestock, and on all the labor of your hands." Haggai 1:9-11.

It is clear that God actually works AGAINST us when we break the law of the increase? When we do not tithe – we are under a curse. God works against the work of our hands. We think we should have a lot – but it's like we have holes in our pockets. We are dissatisfied and unhappy with what we have – even though we make a lot of money. But when we keep this law – little is much, when God is in it. We can have very little in the

THE DAY AFTER LIFE

world's eyes – and yet have so much. Wealth is more an attitude than it is a thing.

Some people say they can't afford to tithe. You can't afford NOT to tithe. The less you have and the more you need – the more important it is to tithe. You want God to bless you – not curse you.

Tithing is simply giving God 10% of what He gives you.

The last law is the "Law of the Harvest." God says, "Do not be deceived: God cannot be mocked. People reap what they sow." Galatians 6:7.

"Cast your bread upon the waters: And after many days it will come back to you." Ecclesiastics 11:1.

The law of the harvest is "what you sow – that is what you will reap". If you sow kindness – that is what you will receive. If you sow love – you will receive a life of love. If you are generous – it will come back to you.

Someone said we all pretty much get what we deserve. I'm not sure if that's accurate or not – but believe we receive what we sow. What we plant as seed will sprout up as experience in our lives. What you sow – that is what you will reap.

(As extracted from wwwq.gotquestions.org/spiritual-laws.html)

THE DAY AFTER LIFE

CHAPTER 2

THE DAY BEFORE

THE DIPLOMAT

When the elevator stopped Marques smiled and said, "Mr. Frye, Harold Frye, this is your stop are you ready for your new future?" Harold looked at Marques and smiled and said, 'All five million dollars of it" and he proceeded towards the elevator doors as they slowly opened. Harold saw that the hallway he was about to enter into was dark except for a glimmer of a flashing exit sign in the distance. Marques smiled and said, "Do not be afraid, Harold Frye, you are in good hands. The lights are motion sensitive once you step into the hallway and move the lights will come up. Go on man, step lively."

Marques laughed a big laugh and Harold stepped out into the dark hallway as the elevator doors closed behind him. Just before the doors fully closed the hallway lights came up and it was suddenly bright as a summer day on the beach. That was when Harold noticed that the hallway was a lot longer then he had thought. It looked as though the hallway went on for miles and miles in each direction. Suddenly he noticed two doors in front of him: a great Oak door and a great Birch wood door, both standing next to the each other.

On the right was the Great Oak Door which was as smooth as glass with no hardware or handle to open it with. The Great

THE DAY AFTER LIFE

Birch door stood on the left and was beautifully adorn with streaks of gold inlaid braids and a massive door handle made from a single cut diamond.

Harold examined both doors closely and then pondered the situation. He wondered why such a great difference between the only two doors in sight. Then he decided to go through the Great Birch door. He just had to feel the touch of the cut diamond handle and since he was about to receive such a substantial honorarium it was only fitting he entered in by way of the door most befitting of his award.

As soon as Harold grabbed the cut diamond door handle his whole life flashed right before his eyes.

Back on the Elevator

When the elevator doors closed behind Harold, Marques turned to the remaining guest's and said, "Did you notice a hint of bitterness in the air?" Each of the passengers looked at each other with a confused look on their faces and nodded no. Then Marques said, "It reminds me of a verse from the book of Ephesians the fourth chapter verses 30 to 34 from the King James Bible: '30 And do not grieve the Holy Spirit of God, by whom you were sealed for the day of redemption. 31 Let all bitterness, wrath, anger, clamor, and evil speaking be put away from you, with all malice. 32 And be kind to one another, tenderhearted, forgiving one another, even as God in Christ forgave you.'" Then he looked around into the faces of each of the remaining passengers smiled and said, "You didn't taste that did you?" Then he laughed a loud laugh and the elevator started to move again.

Back in the Hallway with Harold Frye

Harold found himself standing in a rather bland looking conference room. There were no doors, walls or windows yet he knew it was a conference room. The room was bright yet there were no lights or lamps. Then suddenly in walked a tall thin man with a small goatee in a white suit with a white shirt and tie, and white shoes and socks. He was followed by a younger man who seemed to be carrying the older man's briefcase. The younger man was similarly dressed but he had no goatee.

From the other side of the room a man walked in carrying a small white leather looking portfolio. He was wearing a blue suit, white shirt, blue tie, black shoes, and was clean shaven.

Each of the men sat down in a white chair, at the same time; with the first two sitting across the table from the other. No one sat more than four seats away from the single red chair that stood just in front of where Harold was standing.

The first man to arrive, had his young assistant place his briefcase on the conference table, open it, take out a notebook and turn to a specific page. Then he sat it in front of him as if he did not want to touch it. Then the man in blue quietly opened his portfolio and put on his reading glasses and began to read to himself.

The man in white with the goatee nodded at the man in blue as if signaling him to proceed.

THE DAY AFTER LIFE

But the gentleman in blue continued to review his notes. Then the younger assistant reached in his inside suit jacket pocket and pulled out an envelope and slide it across the table just close enough for it to come to a rest in front of where Harold was still standing behind the red chair. When it came to rest Harold reached and picked it up. It had his name on it so he opened it. At this point no one has said one word.

When Harold opened the letter he saw that there was a bank check in it in the amount of $5 million dollars payable to Cash with his name noted on the memo line. Harold smiled and said, "Thank you." The young man smiled and nodded.

Then the man in blue, with the portfolio spoke and said, "Please make yourself comfortable and have a seat. Mr. Frye or Harold if I may, my name is Louis Fowler and I have a few questions about your intentions concerning the honorarium you just received. If you would now give me your full attention I would appreciate it.

Harold sat down, smiled and said, "Of course."

Then Louis said, "Harold you were born April 21, 1962. You are married to your wife Linda for 30 years. You have three children, Harold Jr., Mark Anthony, and Linda Jr. You live in the East Hampton on Long Island and you work as a Deputy Diplomat at the Office of the United Nations in midtown Manhattan. You recently returned from a diplomatic mission to the Philippines and you have plans to retire later this year or as soon as your son Harold Jr. finishes his studies at your old alma martyr, when he could be considered as your replacement in

THE DAY AFTER LIFE

the diplomatic core. Am I correct so far?"

Harold nodded and said, "Yes all of that is correct. It has been a long standing family tradition that Frye men work in the diplomatic core. We are very proud of Harold Jr. for wanting to follow in the family's tradition of public service."

Louis looked over his reading glasses and said, "Is that so?" Harold taken aback for a moment continued to smile and said, "Yes, Sir. And may I ask why this information is pertinent?"

Louis smiled and said, "No, you may not. We are here to determine the next step for you. You do realize that to one much is given, much is required? We just want to make sure that, you understand what is required of you. And quite frankly Mr. Frye we are very concerned about what you plan to do with our honorarium. Or at least I am. I'll let my colleague across the table make Ns own determination in a moment."

Now a little concerned, Harold responded and said, "I was under the impression that this honorarium was a gift that I might do what I pleased with it. There was no indication that there were any proviso's or stipulations attached to it; otherwise I might just reconsider my acceptance."

Louis smile and said, "This is exactly why you were selected for such a substantial award sir. It seems that over your life you have always looked out for your best interest first and never the interest of other."

Harold now becoming uncomfortable said, "I take exception to that sir, I have lived a very charitable life and been quite considerate of my fellow man."

Louis smiled and said, "Oh! Really sir? Isn't it true that the only reason you make substantial charitable gifts, specifically to your brother-in-laws homeless shelter and church, is to lower your taxable income? And isn't it true that the men your brother-in-law houses at his shelter are routinely used to maintain your gardens and landscaping as well as provide handy man services around your home?"

Harold now beginning to become very uncomfortable smiled and said, "You have that all wrong, many of the men at my brother-in-laws shelter are required to do community service under their probation arrangements and my brother-in-law has found it difficult to place these people with homeowners who sometimes fear they maybe taken advantage of or even robbed."

Then Louis said, "So let's talk about income tax planning; why is it necessary to write off hotel stays, lavish dinners and gifts for your Chief of Staffs sexual favors? Wouldn't it be more accurate to just name her as a dependent? Or would your wife not approve?"

With that Harold turned beet red but before he could say a word, Louis continued and said, "But let's talk about your retirement plans and your son, Harold Jr. Particularly your hopes of Harold Jr. replacing you in the diplomatic service. Isn't it true that your son has told you on numerous occasions that he wasn't interested in joining the diplomatic core and that you had to pull as many strings as possible to box him into a corner

THE DAY AFTER LIFE

leaving him no other option but to join the Diplomatic core? But before you answer that please enlighten us about your plan to stifle your three year unpaid interns hopes of replacing you in the diplomatic core just so you guarantee there would be an opening for your son?"

Harold now very uncomfortable attempted to address the allegations but he was interrupted by Louis once again.

Louis continued to smile and said, "Hold on, none of that is really relevant for these proceedings. Let's cut to the chase here. Please just tell us why you have done everything in your power to keep the Subic Bay Military installation in the Philippines when you know there is no strategic need for it there and that the people of that country do not want it there. And don't tell us, it is because the President has given you, your matching orders and you are just doing what you were told to do."

Harold sat up and said, "Sir I take exception to this line of questioning. Not one word of any of your allegations is true. And I will not dignify any of them with a response."

After Harold's out burst both Louis and his colleague turned around and faced what seemed to be a wall at the far end of the conference table were suddenly a very large television screen appeared. What appeared on the screen started off as if someone had just loaded a 8 miller media film reel and all of the up front markings had to run through before the show actually started. When it did everyone in the room saw and heard a video of Harold plotting and scheming to do each of the deeds

THE DAY AFTER LIFE

Louis had just accused him of; live and in living color. When the video started to run scenes of Harold and Rita having sex Louis stopped it by saying that is enough.

Harold quietly sat back in his chair and slumped down. Then everyone turned back around and faced him. Louis said, "Let me sum up my case here Mr. Frye. I know that the money Charities Unlimited has honored you with is going to a selfish, bitter small minded man and I have just proven it; just by what you have done in the past."

Louis leaned close to the conference room table and placed his elbows on it in front of him and said, "Isn't it true, that you would rather see the people of the Philippines suffer continued moral decay as present day economic hostages to the drug fueled, sexual depravity of drunken American sailors and other military personnel stationed there, because you are ashamed and bitter about the fact that you have several half brothers and sisters of Pilipino decent. Outcast fathered by your grandfather when he was stationed over there?"

The room already silent became as cold as ice for a moment. Harold sat stunned by Louis' statements but there wasn't anything he could say because he knew that Louis was right and he didn't want to see or hear of the scenes from his past concerning statements or thoughts about his siblings in the Philippines. By now Harold was thoroughly embarrassed and ashamed.

Then Louis sat back, closed his portfolio, took a deep breath and said, "May case against Harold Frye is simple. Harold Frye is not representative of those principals and ideals that underpin the spirit and or philosophy that Charities Unlimited has become known for. I say… No; I have proven that Mr. Frye is the epitome of an unforgiving, bitter and angry man, full of hidden resentment and hatred for people." Then Louis sat back in his chair.

Then the young man who carried the briefcase of the man wearing the goatee stood up and said, "Here ye, here ye, here ye Apostle Jeremiah will now begin his query of Harold Frye, everyone come to order and hear what is to be." As soon as he finished he sat back down.

Apostle Jeremiah cleared his throat and said, "I'm not sure if the gentleman on the other side of the table had a chance to set the record straight for this query but let me proceed with my query and we can set the record straight when I have finished. First let me honor the Most High and give thanks for this opportunity to meet you Mr. Frye. My associate and I will attempt to clear up or set the record straight concerning the points that have been leveled against you thus far. Further inquiry into those and other matters may or may not be required of you later."

Harold sat up in his seat in preparation to speak and Apostle Jeremiah looked at him and said, "There is no need to speak right now, there will be plenty of time for that when you are finished here." And although Harold tried and tried to interrupt by speaking he could not utter a word or even make a gesture, so finally he just sat back and quietly listened.

Then Apostle Jeremiah pulled the notebook his assistant had sat before, closer and began to read.

He said, "In the matter of your son, Harold Jr. let the record note that Harold Jr.'s destiny does not rest in his father's efforts or lack thereof. It is noted that Harold Sr. loves his son dearly, even more than life itself and only wants the best for him and his future."

Jeremiah continued and said, "And in the matter of Harold Sr.'s adulterous activities, which have been countless in nature, it should be noted that unbeknownst to him, he is, and I will address this issue further in a moment, under a generational curse. That is, his father and his fore fathers before him were under a family curse that was leveled on their great, great, great, grandfather for sins of the heart he committed before any of the forefathers were conceived. Since Harold Sr. did not know of the curse and did not find himself in a position to know, that would be by attending a Holy Ghost filled Bible based church, that charge can not be attached to him.

Now let me move to the single most important concern offered by the gentleman across the table from me, that of 'Unforgiveness, bitterness, anger, resentment, hatred and jealousy for his Philippine American siblings and by extension the Philippine peoples.'

Right here a little background may help. Mr. Frye believes he is a descendent of an African American male and an Asian American woman, and thus has a unique sensitivity and compassion for people of the Asian culture. Thus on the one hand it would seem hypercritical of him to hold any kind of

THE DAY AFTER LIFE

dislike for his Phillippino relatives as well as the Phillippino peoples. However man's heart is a deceitful thing and harbors' sin and evil. What Mr. Frye does not know, even in light of his expensive genealogical certifications, is that he too is of Phillippino decent. Mr. Frye your great, great, great, great grandfather and mother were of pure Phillippino blood, he a prince and she his princess. And through intercultural marriages both Phillippino, white and Black bloodlines are carried in you. This information was not available to your genealogical researchers but our records date back much further and are much more accurate.

But my concern here is not the truth's that you knew or didn't knew. My concern is that you find pleasure in harboring the spirits of resentment, unforgiveness, bitterness, anger and hatred for people. You have a desire to live as if you are better than others. There is where I want to start my query, please respond."

Harold took a deep breath and realized that he could now speak so he pondered what he would say for a moment and then said, "Sir! I am not sure who either of you two are, or what this line of questioning has to do with this award. However I am willing to indulge you to a point and right now I have heard quite enough of these insulting and baseless innuendos and falsehoods. Now if either of you have the power to resend this award I beg you do so for I have answered all of the questions I intend to answer for either of you. Good day." And he started to get up to leave.

THE DAY AFTER LIFE

When he stood up and turned to leave he realized that there was no door behind him, or window; so after turning and looking around a couple of times he finally said, "Where is the exit?"

Apostle Jeremiah smiled and said, "Why don't you return to your seat for a moment and let me explain how this works." Harold reluctantly returned to his seat, sat down and attentively listened.

When Apostle Jeremiah saw that Harold had relaxed and settled down, he turned to the wall, as did Louis and his assistant, where the video screen had appeared earlier. As it seemingly powered up Apostle Jeremiah said, "Let me show you something before we get to the explanation on exiting this discussion. But first this family tree might help to clear up a few things. Notice here that every name listed on this first screen is familiar to you. I'm not going to sit here and name names because I know you know all of the names shown here as well as the faces. This next screen shows you all of those members of your father's generation. Now some of these people you not only don't know but you have never seen before yet I assure you, they are in your bloodline. Now the next four hundred screens chronicle your entire family lineage back to Adam and Eve. Yes that far back, I'm not going to show you the faces or names of who they are or who is to come because there will be plenty of time for you to learn about and to meet them after this.

Oh! Yes. That is right, however the only question that would

THE DAY AFTER LIFE

need to be answered now is from what position will you be learning about and or hearing about or meeting them from?"

Then Apostle Jeremiah turned back to Harold who was sitting in awe as his family lineage flashed across the screen, when he saw the final slide, that of Adam and Eve his mouth dropped on the conference table and as the light blub flickered in between his eyes, Apostle Jeremiah said, "Yes Harold that was Adam and his wife Eve. And yes, you are dead."

Then Harold teetered over in his chair and fell on the conference table face first. After about two or three minutes he regained consciousness and sat back up. And in a low quiet voice Harold said, "I'm dead? When? How? Why me?"

Apostle Jeremiah smiled and said, "All I can say is that God finally found time to meet with you. Right now you are being screened to see if you should meet with him and if so what area or areas you should concentrate on for your meeting with the Most High. It's my century to represent the Lord at the screening table as well as Mr. Fowlers shift to represent the Enemy. Now with that said, "I want to remind you as to where we left off at, in hopes of getting your response before this session expires. Please if you will?"

Harold quietly said, "Would you repeat the question, please, sir?"

Apostle Jeremiah took a deep breath and said, "My question was, do you find pleasure in harboring the spirits of resentment, unforgiveness, bitterness, anger and hatred for people. And do

THE DAY AFTER LIFE

you have a desire to live as if you are better than others?"

The day before receiving notice of his honorarium from Charities Unlimited, Harold Frye the career diplomat with the United Nations attached to the Southwest Asia envoy could not be a happier man. He was closer to retiring then ever before, his son was about to be notified that a summer internship with the diplomatic core was approved and he had just had the most successful meeting of his career as lead negotiator with the Phillippine government concerning the continued leasing and expansion of the Subic Bay military facility there.

Harold was looking forward to returning home, later in the day, now that his two week marathon of negotiations had finally concluded.

Harold had planned to have lunch with his chief of staff Rita Lowenstein at the American Embassy in the Philippines at noon and then spend a little quality time with her before his flight back to the states.

Seated at their usual table in the back of the cafeteria, Harold waited for Rita to arrive. Usually she was very prompt and prone to notify him if she was going to be even a minute late. That, other than her youthful attitude and athletic figure were the things Harold admired most about her, other than the fact that she was a trusted confident.

But this afternoon was to be one for the record book. Harold's lunch date was for 12:00 noon sharp and at 12:30pm when Rita had not shown or called he became concerned so he called

THE DAY AFTER LIFE

Rita's cellphone but there was no answer. So he called her desk and his message went straight to voice mail. Another 15 minutes slipped by and Harold decided to return to the office and see what was keeping her. He paid his check and left using the most direct route to his office just in case he would run into Rita running late.

When Harold stepped off of the elevator he noticed his office door was a jar, which was a strict no, no for security reasons. In the event the compounds security was breached, entry to locked personal offices would be consider the second line of defense as well as an additional deterrent.

Harold cautiously approached the open door and the first thing he noticed was a sealed FedEx envelope addressed to him on the floor just inside the open office door. He assumed it was slide under the office door sometime during the day. Then he noticed while it was the middle of the day, all of the interior office lights were off.

As Harold pushed the door open to enter the office he met strong resistance, as if something was holding the door in place or behind it. When he looked around the door to see what was hindering the door from smoothly opening he saw Rita's bare leg with her stockings pulled down around her ankle. Harold immediately recoiled and started to call Rita's name as he pushed his way in to see what had happened to her.

When he got inside the office he turned on the office lights and he could see that there had been some kind of a struggle. Harold called out for help and many of his colleagues began to step outside of their offices and come to his aid. Harold bent over Rita and checked for her pulse and determined there was none. By then two of his colleagues had arrived and said security was on its way. One of the bystanders suggested that Harold step back because he was disturbing the crime scene and when he attempted to get up he put his hand in a pool of blood that was covered by her hair to make matters worse, he in advertently wiped the thick fluid on his shirt and pants before he even thought about it.

That's when Chief of Security Walter Rice stepped through the crowd and into the room, followed by his second in command as well as the embassy press core.

Chief Rice immediately assessed the situation in his own mind and had his men lock down the embassy and escort the press core and the onlookers away from the crime scene. Then he asked Harold to stay and wait outside the office in the hallway.

When everyone had been sent away or pushed back as far as possible Chief Rice asked Harold to wait outside of the office while he and his men examined the crime scene. After what seemed like an hour, Chief Rice stepped out of the office and allowed the forensic team to step in and do their job. But before the Chief began to question Harold, he told his second in command to call the Philippine Minister of Police and ask him to bring his investigative team over for a briefing. Then he walked over to Harold and asked if he could talk to him for a few minutes.

Chief Rice, Harold Frye and the Chief's second in charge stepped

THE DAY AFTER LIFE

across the hallway into one of the empty offices and sat down to talk.

Inside the office Harold was visibly shaken and upset. Chief Rice asked if he wanted or needed anything to calm his nerves and Harold said no thanks. Harold continued to murmur 'who could have done this to Rita?'

Finally Chief Rice responded and said, "That is exactly the question I need you to answer." Harold had a strange look on his face when he looked up at the Chief and said, "I don't like your tone Chief. What is that supposed to mean?" Chief Rice said, "I didn't stutter did I? I want to know from you if there was any reason someone would want your Chief of Staff brutally killed? This wasn't some kind of a random burglary gone wrong someone deliberately breached two levels of embassy security, risked getting caught or even shot, took the time to sexually assault a high level employee, and then purposively ram sake a government office looking for only God knows what. Then they manage to escape without breaching the same security protocols again. Now if this is not an inside job, which I doubt, it had to be a bit more than random, don't you think?"

Harold blankly stirred at the Chief for a moment, and then the Chief pointed at the Harold and said, "What is that?" Harold looked down and saw Rita's blood smeared all over his shirt and pants, then he looked at his right and saw some more blood on it as well and said, "I must of gotten it on me when I checked her for a pulse?" Chief Rice responded and said, "I saw you do that from behind the crowd, I'm talking about that FedEx envelope in your other hand. What's that?"

That was when Harold realized he was still holding the FedEx envelope that he'd picked up when he stepped inside his office and found Rita's body. Harold looked at it and said, "I found this on the floor by my door when I came up to see what was keeping Rita. We had planned to have lunch together earlier. At noon but by 12:300pm I got worried, so I started back up to the office to see what was keeping her. I'm scheduled to fly back to the states this evening and I wanted to discuss something's before I left."

Chief Rice said, "So open it and see what it's about." Harold looked at the envelope and said, "It's un-open and addressed to me what does this have to do with anything?" Chief Rice said, "It may have everything to do with this. Don't you want to know what's in it? Or do you already know what's in it?" Harold said, "Judging by the name of the sender, 'Charities Unlimited' in New York, it is probably a tax receipt or a personal thank you for one of my many charitable contributions. I'll open when I feel like it and not before. However in the spirit of cooperation if there is anything remotely relevant to this situation you will be the first to know if I find anything of interest, sir."

Chief Rice smiled and sat back, then he said, "Need I remind you that this is a murder investigation in a foreign country but for all intents and purposes on U.S. soil. Which puts it right smack within the confines of my soul jurisdiction? You will open that letter now or we will restrain you, confiscate it, then open it and hold it, as evidence in this investigation until its ultimate

THE DAY AFTER LIFE

resolution or not."

Harold drew a deep breath, leaned into Chief Rice's face and said, "Need I remind you of who I am, sir? I am the senior attaché and you report to me. I don't report to you." Chief Rice smiled again and said, "In the event of a security breach of any magnitude, sir. I report to the President of the United States or in his absence the National Security Advisor, not you. Now hand it over or open it up."

Reluctantly, Harold handed the envelope over to the Chief and said, "Remind me to make a note in your permanent file about your tone, and arrogant attitude when this over." As Chief Rice opened the envelope he smiled and said, "Better yet I'll remind the President to remind you, when I make my report about your lack of cooperation in this matter. Oh! And I will certainly make a point to alert him of your ongoing sexual affair with your Chief of Staff. In the meantime I hope you read up or become familiar with the morals' clause in your oath of office. And maybe take a look at the government's rules on sexual misconduct between an appointed officials and members of their or anyone else's staff. I guess when the old man gets a ear full of that we'll see whose permanent file gets a note or not, sir."

Then Chief Rice read he took out of the FedEx envelope out loud and for the benefit of his second in command and Harold. The letter notified Harold that he had been selected as the organizations Philanthropher of the year and that he was encouraged to stop by at his earliest convenience to retrieve his $5 million dollar honorarium. Chief Rice was in awe. Both he

THE DAY AFTER LIFE

and his deputy profusely apologized but reconfirmed that it was a necessary part of their investigation and their duty to inspect any and all material that might be relevant to the investigation regardless of its owner or its content. Harold smugly reiterated his plan to make note of the incident in the Chief's file first chance he got.

MABLE SHELBORNE

When the elevator arrived at Mable's floor, Marques announced her name as the doors opened. A great rush of thick white fog appeared in the elevator doorway as Mable stepped out into the hallway. As the elevator doors closed behind her, the lights came up and the brightness of the hallway was almost blinding. Mable wiped her eyes and looked at the two great doors in front of her.

The oak door was on her right and the birch door was on her left. At first she wondered which one belonged to the Charity, but before she could step towards either, the birch door suddenly disappeared right in front of her eyes. Only the oak door remained.

 Mable reached out and touched the great oak door, and she, too, saw her recent life pass in front of her eyes like a television movie in fast forward. ... All six of her children were living with her, until the eldest, a twenty-two year old twin daughter, abruptly moved out. This was a surprise. Mable's eldest daughters, Shay and Clarice, had weathered their life of poverty just fine. They had both walked the straight and narrow road

THE DAY AFTER LIFE

nearly their whole lives.

Mable had done the best she could in raising her children under difficult circumstances. She had also lived from hand to mouth most of her life, living down the hall from her grandmother in the same housing complex for many years. At age eighteen, she got her own apartment with her three children and life seemed to be one long wait for a change-- a change for the better.

Mable, although a church-going, God-fearing woman, had made her share of mistakes, but all for the right reasons, if that is possible. It wasn't her fault that every man she ever loved was either, a common criminal, dope addict, dope dealer, or just a wannabe ladies' man. She just couldn't help herself, and she never really learned how to cope with loneliness until she hit age forty.

Shay and Clarice's father, William, was a military man. Just before the birth of the girls, his tour of duty at Fort Hamilton ended, and William was told he would be reassigned. The only question was where he would be reassigned.

 When he was notified that he was being sent to Korea, Mable was flabbergasted. She just never expected him to have to leave the country, and to add insult to injury, after his one-year tour ended, Mable discovered that William had found a wife before he returned state-side. The good news was, he never forgot his daughters, and would always send money to them even though he never visited. He did keep in touch by letter and occasionally by phone.

THE DAY AFTER LIFE

Mable's other children never spoke a word of envy, but Mable knew the look in their eyes when Shay and Clarice's father would send a check for their school supplies. Those looks of, 'why doesn't my father ever think to send me money?' just broke her heart. So, early on Mable learned to make it a point to spread the twins' allowance around as much as she could. Social Services did what they could with the other children's fathers, but with child support payments there was always some new excuse why the money either never showed up or was late in coming.

Over the years, Mable had become just as astute as her mother, and her grandmother before her, making ends meet while living from welfare check to welfare check. She learned how to shop at the thrift store, and attend every church swap meet, to keep the children from knowing how hard things really were.

But through it all Mable made a point to be at church every Sunday, come rain or shine, and bring an offering, even if only a dollar. With children in tow you could count on Sister Mable being in the front pew for Sunday school and the last row for choir rehearsal. Pastor Thomas would always say, "No one could hold a bass note like Sister Mable."

Then last Monday morning it was like all hell had broken out in the Shelborne apartment. The mailman came and brought both good and bad news. First it was a letter from Old Westbury College addressed to Clarice, granting her a full scholarship to their School of Education. When Clarice read the letter everyone broke out in screams of joy. She was the first in five

THE DAY AFTER LIFE

generations, as far back as anyone could remember, who was ever accepted into college. Mable was so proud of her eldest daughter, and deep down in her soul she knew Clarice was destined for something better in life than what she could offer her. Like any other day in the life of the Shelborne household, when something good happened, something bad was just waiting around the corner.

As expected the mail brought troubling news that day as well. Shay received a letter from the OB-GYN doctor at the free health clinic that same morning saying that she was six weeks pregnant, with twins. On the surface that news was a blessing. However, without even knowing who the father was, and Shay being the only one in the family working--a part-time job at that-- this blessing was quickly labeled a burden. Mable made arrangements to have her younger sons move furniture around so the babies would be comfortable when they arrived, and she called and made plans to meet with the Pastor of the church to discuss helping her find a part-time job to replace Shay's income. Mable always said, "Never wait until trouble knocked on the door, when you know it's on the way."

The next morning, Tuesday, Mable was ready to take on another challenge; this round would literally be more than she ever expected. Seated at the breakfast table that morning, while Mable prepared the young ones' breakfasts and school lunches, was Clarice. Seated next to her on the floor was her suitcase, and it seemed to be stuffed with everything she ever owned.

THE DAY AFTER LIFE

Walking over to the refrigerator, Mable looked at Clarice and her suitcase and said, "Good morning and what gets you up so early, you moving out?"

Clarice stood up, grabbed her suitcase and said, "Damn, Skippy, I'm out! And just so you know I'm so glad I can hardly contain myself. If I never see these projects or your broke ass ever again it will be too soon."

It seemed like Mable's jaw dropped to her knees as her heart fell to the floor. She was so shocked and surprised Clarice would say such things to her that she didn't know whether the child was possessed or if she were dreaming. Mable just stood there frozen in time and watched as Clarice slammed her house keys down on the kitchen table and said, "Here, take these-- you can give them to the next rug rat the milk man drops off-- I won't be needing them." Then she continued to walk towards the front door and as she opened it, she said, "Oh! Yeah, I almost forgot; don't call me until, I call you ...that will be, oh right, never." Then she slammed the door closed behind her.

Mable stood in the middle of the kitchen and broke down crying for an hour until the last of her children had left for school. But even in the midst of her tears she never stopped praying that Clarice would be all right, wherever she was going.

Shortly after Mable finished crying, her daughter Shay walked into the kitchen and took one look at her and said, "Ma, what is wrong with you?"

Mable welled up again but she held back the tears this time and

THE DAY AFTER LIFE

with a smile on her face she said, "Me and the Lord were just talking about how all grown up Clarice and you are, that's all." Then she made breakfast for Shay.

When Shay finished eating she said, "Ma you can fool some people all of the time but I ain't one of them. What's going on with you this morning? Are we getting put out-- again?"

Mable smiled and said, "No, baby I'm just happy for you and Clarice; matter a fact, Clarice left early this morning to start school."

Shay became angry and said, "So she left without even saying goodbye to us?"

Mable started to respond but right then there was a knock at the front door. Mable looked out the peephole and told Shay that it was a Federal Express courier with an   envelope. When she opened the door to sign for the delivery, she asked Shay to bring her pocketbook for a tip, but the man smiled and said, "That's not necessary, mama."

Shay handed Mable her pocketbook and she reached inside and pulled out her last $5.00 bill, folded it up and pushed it into the man's hand as she returned the signed clipboard. Then she said, "It's not a problem. I appreciate your coming all the way up here. Please take it and have a cup of coffee on me." Then she slowly closed and locked the door.

By the time Mable had returned to the kitchen table to sit down and read the express letter, Shay had asked a million questions. Just the two of them were home as Mable opened the letter and handed it to Shay to read while she searched in her pocketbook for her reading glasses.

After reading the letter to herself for a minute, Shay began to holler and scream, ..."Praise the Lord, praise the Lord, and praise the Lord!"

Mable reached over and grabbed the letter from her hand to read out loud. By the time she got to the words, 'One Hundred Thousand' she was speechless and could not even form the word 'dollars' with her mouth. Finally, Mable got hold of herself and grabbed Shay around the mouth and said, "Quiet, quiet, girl, get a hold of yourself. This is probably one of those 'Ponzo-be' schemes. You know like down on Wall Street."

When Shay heard that, she busted out laughing and said, "Ma, you crazy. You mean Punzi schemes? I don't think so. These people are for real, for real. You see them on the news all the time just giving money away to good people. I sent them a letter a few weeks ago telling them about you and all the good work you do at the church, and Pastor Thomas signed it. He said you were the greatest volunteer ever, Ma. I guess they believed us."

Mable said, "The letter says I can come down anytime and pick up the money. What do you think I should do?"

"Duh...go downtown and pick up the money, ya think?"

"I can't," Mable answered.

"What you mean you can't? You better get down there and

THE DAY AFTER LIFE

pick that money up, today! -- Even if I got to carry you, for real, for real."

"You may have to carry me-- I just gave that delivery man my last five dollars and that was all the money had between me and the 15th. Child I'm so broke even I can't pay attention."

"Look Ma, I have ten dollars bus fare for the week. You go get that money. I'll call Jeffrey and get the money back for my bus fare."

"Jeffrey? The Youth Pastor? Is he your baby's daddy? I thought you didn't know who the baby daddy was," Mable said.

"I didn't want to say anything at first, not until I knew what--if anything-- he was going to do. He called me last night and asked me to marry him. I said yes. Then we agreed to surprise everybody and tell y'all at church on Sunday. So here... take this, and you go on and get that bus into the city and get that money, you deserve it..." Shay smiled.

Later that morning as Mable got on the N-39 bus to Manhattan all she could think of was why me, Lord? What did I do to deserve all of this? She wondered what the Pastor said to compel those people to give her so much money, money. What was she going to do with all that money? By the time Mable got to the Chrysler Building in Midtown, she had decided she wasn't worthy of so much money and was just going to tell them thanks but no thanks.

Then she thought-- what about the children? It would be much easier on them if they could get new clothes instead of used, or if they could have bologna instead of peanut butter for lunch, and she just became more and more confused.

On the elevator, when Mable was asked why she thought she was selected to be honored, she took a deep breath, smiled and said, "God only knows, but my daughter and my Pastor wrote a letter and here I am."

PASTOR WILLIE JACKSON

The morning before Pastor Jackson's award arrived was not typical in anyway shape or form at all. The morning started out poorly and unbeknownst to him, if not for his receiving the Charities Unlimited award letter by messenger later that evening, the day was destine to end just as poorly as it started.

Pastor Jackson had schedule two very important meetings for that morning and had planned to start his day at sunrise or as close to 6:00am as possible. Not realizing how tired he really was after the weekends much needed church revival. When Pastor Jackson laid down the night before at around midnight and did not wake until 8:30am when he was scheduled to preside over the 8:00am Senior Clergy monthly breakfast, was the first sign of a day that wasn't going to go well. Pastor Jackson had planned to host the monthly Senior Clergy breakfast meeting with the local district City Councilman as guest speaker. To make matters worse Pastor Jackson himself was also on the agenda to not only introduce the guest speaker but to give remarks afterwards.

Only by the grace of God did he get dressed and leave Rockville

THE DAY AFTER LIFE

Center, Long Island and make it to 128th Street and 7th Ave. by 9:45am. Then he spent most of the remaining minutes of the breakfast meeting apologizing for his lateness. Not wanting to rush off; but his second scheduled meeting with the church legal counsel at 11:00am. That meant he had to get all the way from central Harlem to Bay Shore, which was an hours drive at best, on a good day. Calling ahead he rescheduled the meeting for 11:30am so he would be on time. Although the reality was he was on time but he had less time to go over the issues he desperately needed to.

Pastor Jackson had a few financial problems in both his ministry and his personal life, more perplexing was the fact that the seemed to stem from the same problem.

While things were going well as far as collections coming in to the church, it just seemed that there was never enough to make ends meet. Things started to come to a head about three months earlier when the bank notified him at his home, that they had filed a foreclosure notice on it, as well as the church building. It seemed that the mortgages on both properties were behind almost $75,000 in total.

Now Pastor Jackson wasn't the church treasurer but he did sign all checks and make all of the deposits so he couldn't for the life of him, figure out why the mortgage was so far behind. He knew he hadn't spent the money so he tried to discreetly find out were the cash drain was. A few weeks ago he met and talked with his accountant about this and they came up with a plan to catch whoever was stealing from the church. Because the church was growing so fast the church Elders decided that Sunday services had to be increased from one to three. And since people were coming especially to hear Pastor Jackson's weekly message he could no longer keep his eye on the money and focus on the people at the same time as he'd done in the past. So the accountant suggested that he plant marked bills in the offering plate to see if they showed up in the bank deposit. That didn't work; it was too much of a long shot. Then after several weeks of trying that and the foreclosure notice had come, the accountant realized that the problem wasn't a weekly pilfering of the collection plate, but the problem was much more sinister in nature. He found out that someone had gotten a hold of the Pastors personal information and had taken out a third mortgage on both properties unbeknownst to both him and the church Elders. But he concluded that at least one church Elder had to know.

Church Elder Dent the president of the Elders board seemed the most likely. Between the accountant and the church attorney they figured out how the transaction was pulled off and who was most likely to have knowingly involved in it or planned it. More than $200,000.00 had been drawn down on a secret third mortgage and funneled into Elder Dents personal accounts. The attorney had both video and audio of Elder Dent moving the stolen funds from one bank account to another on several occasions.

Today's meeting was to discuss the options in front of Pastor Jackson as Pastor of the Church, Pastor Jackson the citizen and

THE DAY AFTER LIFE

Pastor Jackson the Chairman of the Church Elder Board.

The meeting with the attorney went far longer than Pastor Jackson ever imagined. Not only was his attorney long winded but he was quite thorough and he had asked one of the police detectives and a prosecutor for the New York County District Attorney's office to attend the lunch meeting on the churches dime.

By the time Pastor Jackson had gotten out of that so called working lunch meeting it was almost 4:00pm. Although the meeting was very informative Pastor Jackson was still left with making the final decision on his own; whether to have Elder Dent arrested and thrown in jail on felony identity theft charges for 3 to 5 years or come up with $200,000 before the bank padlocked the church and sat him out in the street.

By the time Pastor Jackson had gotten out of the meeting his head was spinning and he still had to make it back to Harlem to attend the churches weekly Bible Study class and the monthly Board of Elders meeting.

At 7:30pm Pastor Jackson had made his way back into Manhattan and was on his way uptown to Harlem and Bible study. He had given both his and the churches financial situation a great deal of thought by now and he had decided to convene a full board intercessory prayer session before he opened his mouth on the subject of the foreclosure. Elder Dents faith rested in the moment between the ending of the corporate prayer and the moment he opened his mouth again. Pastor Jackson was emotionally torn to the point of agita and

THE DAY AFTER LIFE

convulsions almost. He blamed himself for not seeing that his friend of almost 30 years was in such financial need that he would resort to identity theft, or that, the spirit of a theft was upon and in him. Pastor Jackson just couldn't believe that he did not see this coming. He wasn't sure what was worst, his best friend's betrayal or him not being foretold by the Holy Spirit that there was a Judas in his camp.

Board of Elders Meeting

As soon as Bible Study ended and the visitors and students walked out the Church Elders walked in and took their seats in preparation for the regular monthly meeting. Pastor Jackson waited outside the conference room until everyone had entered and taken their rightful seat. The seating arrangement wasn't formal but it had become a tradition; Pastor Jackson would sit at the foot of the table, Elder Dent would seat at the head with the Church Treasurer at his right hand and the Church Secretary at his left; everyone else would sit against the wall in side chairs.

When Pastor Jackson walked in last everyone stood to greet him. As they stood and said their hello's Pastor Jackson smiled and bow towards each of them in his usual fashion, a sign of respect and love.

Once that was done but before everyone sat down, Pastor Jackson asked for a corporate prayer with everyone resting on their feet. The prayer was lead by the person closes to Pastor Jackson's right hand and then each came in his or her own way when their turn came. They prayed one after another until it returned to Pastor Jackson for the final prayer and word from

THE DAY AFTER LIFE

the Lord for the evenings meeting.

Pastor Jackson prayed an unusually long prayer, general in nature but specific for guidance in the evenings work. When he finished he asked that everyone remain standing because the word from the Lord was a 'shift' had come to the Church. And as everyone continued to praise God for his word, Pastor Jackson walked up to the head of the conference room table and stood behind Elder Dent momentarily. When Elder Dent realized what had just happened he quietly stepped to the side and went to sit in the Pastor's usual seat at the foot of the table. When Elder Dent made his way around the conference room table to Pastor Jackson's usual seat he looked for acknowledgment from Pastor Jackson and there was none. He waited for a moment and finally Pastor Jackson looked down at the table and shook his head no, and then Elder Dent bowed and left the room. By the time everyone settled down from exalting and praising the Lord Elder Dent had left the board meeting and was outside in the parking lot. Unbeknownst to anyone there at that very moment Elder Dent was being arrested and taken away in handcuffs.

The Close of the Elders Monthly Board Meeting

While Pastor Jackson did not say anything about the day's activities he did advise the board of Elders that there would be a special meeting after Sunday Service and that he expected everyone to attend. Then he led them in a close out prayer and benediction and sent everyone home.

It was 10:00pm when Pastor Jackson stepped out of the church

THE DAY AFTER LIFE

conference room's side door into the side parking lot, when he heard a slight tap on a truck horn. When he turned to see where it came from he saw that there was a FedEx van parked in the driveway with its emergency lights flashing on and off. He shaded his eyes and the driver turned the flashers off, disembarked and ran over waving an express envelope in his hand. Pastor Jackson asked, "Do you know what time it is? I know this must be important for you if you needed to deliver it at this time of night. Who are you looking for?" The courier said, "Pastor Jackson, do you know him?" Pastor Jackson looked at him and said, "Can I sign for it?" The courier said, "Only if you are Pastor Jackson this one is a special delivery sir, I'm sorry." Then Pastor Jackson smiled and said, "I'm Pastor Jackson do you need to see some I.D.?" The courier said, "No sir, your word will do, besides I asked everyone who came out before you and they described you to a 'T'." Then he smiled and handed Pastor Jackson the envelope and his clipboard to sign.

MIKE ABRAHAM

The morning, of the day Mike received notice of his Charities Unlimited honorarium, was like any other morning; up at the crack of noon, shower, brunch at the campus cafeteria and then off to his first class which started at 1:45pm. Mike usually sleeps through the next three classes and is well rested for his usual evening activity-drinking, drugging and chasing co-eds.

Mike doesn't worry about taking notes in class he relies on his frat brothers for that. He knows that the week before any major test, they email him all of the class notes he'll need, to ace the

THE DAY AFTER LIFE

test. His reports and papers are always well researched and written in advance since the fraternity keeps its library of instructor preferences and bias, up to date. The regular parade of pledges that the fraternity entertains are the ones required to keep the library update with relevant thesis, report and papers in all subject matter. Mike had college down to a science until that morning when it seemed all hell broke loose.

At around 5:00pm just after his last class, Mike usually makes a short run uptown to pick up a bag of weed and maybe a couple of vyckadin to make it through the evenings activities, you know just a little somethin, somethin to keep up his social edge. But yesterday was different, Mikes usual dealer, Hoodlum, was unusually anxious when Mike pulled up. There were no words of wisdom, or warnings that drugs would someday stunt his growth, it was just put the money on the ground pull around the corner, and wait for the runner to blow by and drop the goods in the back seat. Mike remembered Hoodlum spoke direct and straight forward.

So as soon as Mike pulled up, Hoodlum pointed to the ground, and waved him off around the corner. Mike started to say something funny, but Hoodlum yelled in a strong low voice, "Move it College Boy, now!" Somewhat insulted Mike drove off and thought nothing of it. No sooner did he park around the corner, did he hear several loud firecrackers explode and then he saw, coming from behind his car Hoodlum, being chased by two men waving guns. Once the three men got a few feet in front of Mike's car he saw Hoodlum trip and fall down, and then one of the two men fire several shots into his back. Finally, one

THE DAY AFTER LIFE

of then walked up to Hoodlum's lifeless body, and drop a gun he took from his waistband, down on the street by his hand and walk back towards the direction they came running from. By then Mike had slid so far down in his seat he looked like a floor mat to the men as they walked by his car.

To afraid to move, Mike waited a few minutes to see what would happen next, as a small crowd started to form. After a couple more minutes there were just too many people standing around Hoodlum's body so Mike felt he was stuck there; and that was when three patrol cars pulled up one of which was unmarked.

Just Mike's luck that the two plain clothes officers in the unmarked car were the two men he had just seem chasing and shooting Hoodlum in the back earlier. Mike started his car and attempted to back up back around the corner. But just as he looked in his rearview mirror, he saw two foot patrol officers walking up behind his car waving him to put it in park. One officer was a tall black male and the other a short black female.

Mike put the car in park and waited for the officers to approach his window. As the two officers got closer Mike noticed that one was coming up on the passenger side and the other on the driver's side. He let the windows down on both sides and politely asked how could he be of service.

The female officer spoke first and said, "How long you been parked here?" Mike responded and said, "Parked here, no. I just pulled up here and saw the crowd. I sat and waited for a minute to see what was going on and then I decided I should just back on out and leave. ...But I really haven't been here long officer, maybe a minute or less. I think I actually pulled around as the other police cars were driving up."

The female officer looked around in Mike's car and said, "Nice car. What year is this?" Mike reluctantly said, "It's a new one, a 0-10." Then she said, "You live around here?" Mike said, "No I was taking a short cut to the NYU campus." Then the other officer said, "You a law student there?" Mike turned and responded to him, "Yes, 3rd year, my fathers an attorney too. It's a family tradition of sorts."

Then the female officer said, "I can tell." Mike turned back to her and said, "Oh! How so?" The female officer smiled and said, "Bad lying must run in the family."

Mike smiled and said, "So what is that supposed to mean? You don't even know me or anyone in my family, officer?"

The other officer said, "We are gonna need you to step out of the car, sir." Mike turned back to him and said, "I beg your pardon, what for?" The officer said, "There seems to be a funny odor coming from inside your car it smells like marijuana. Step out please and place your hands on the hood."

Mike started to say something about harassment but the female officer opened the passenger side door, got in and started to feel around under the passenger seat. Mike said, "You don't have permission to search my car. I know my rights." Then the male officer pulled Mike from inside the car right out of the drivers side window and slammed him on the ground.

THE DAY AFTER LIFE

Before he knew it the plain clothes officers were walking over towards him. Mike got silent. When the two plain clothes officers walked up one of them, the one who planted the gun on Hoodlum said, "What you got here, patrolmen?" The male officer said, "I think this one saw the shooting and he won't cooperate."

Mike could see the plain clothes officer's eye's light up. Then he said, "Is that so?" That was when the female officer stepped out of Mike's car and said, "It's clean except for these seeds and some matches. It looks like his car wash missed a few spots." Then the plain clothes officer said, "Good work officers cuff him and hold him here while I get a bus for that body over there, a tow for this lovely car and a sector car to transport your little student friend here to lock up."

Then he and his partner walked back over to Hoodlum's body and started talking to the coroner who had just arrived.

That was when Mike got so scared he started to cry and wet his pants. When the female officer saw that she said, "What the hell is wrong with you, fool? Harry look at this boy he done wet his pants and look he is crying like a little baby now that those handcuffs are on him. What's the matter baby you need your momma?" Then both officers laughed out loud.

Mike said, "Look, look I'm sorry I was rude but I got to tell you something. I need your help, please. Can I call my dad now? I have to talk to him, right now." The female officer said, "You're a third year law student, who knows his rights; you should know that you don't get a phone call until you've been processed at

THE DAY AFTER LIFE

the station and given your rights which are as follows." And she began to read him his rights. By now Mike is beside himself and he knows that if he goes down town with the two officers that shot Hoodlum in the back and planted that gun there is no way he'll survive the trip. So he continued to plead with the female officer to listen to him for just one minute.

Finally, when she finished reading him his rights she said, "Now we'll see how this mark on your record fairs with you getting a law license, Mr. Smartass. Welcome to the justice system you little prick."

Mike screamed out 'Please, please just listen to me for one minute, please, I beg you.' The male officer said, "This will teach you a listen Smartass, respect, the working man." Then Mike just fell down on his knees and said, "God if they would only hear what I have to say, please lord, please help me."

Then the female officer said, "What do you have to say, fool? If it's anything other than I'm sorry, you are gonna be sorry, I assure you. Speak up!"

Mike said, "Please don't let me go with those other officers I beg you. Promise me, please." The female officer said, "That's ...? What difference does it make?"

Mike said, "I saw them shot Hoodlum in the back and drop a gun next to his hand. I saw them and now they know I saw them. I lied and said, I just pulled up but I was waiting for Hoodlum's runner to drop my dupe. I just pulled up and left $150 dollars, a hundred and a torn fifty that said, 'Life's a Beach'

THE DAY AFTER LIFE

on the back in black magic marker. Hoodlum always has me drop my money on the ground right beside the car, in the street, then drive around here and wait for his runner to come and drop my dupe through my rear seat. But today he was real nervous. Nervous as hell, so I dropped the money and drove around here. But by the time I parked I heard several shots and then I saw Hoodlum running around towards the front of my car. Then those two guys over there, the plain clothes officers, came running behind him shooting. Hoodlum fell down and they walked up on him and shot him three more times in the back. Then the guy who just spoke to me reached in his waistband and pulled out a .25 automatic and dropped it on the street next to Hoodlums hand. Then they walked back around the corner. I slid down in the front seat of my car so they wouldn't see me when they walked pass. Next thing I know there was a crowd and then you guys showed up. Look I don't want to die please, I'll testify. Just don't let them take me."

Both of the officers looked at each other and then they turned away from Mike and spoke in a low voice for a moment. When they turned back around the sector car that was called, pulled up and was ready to transport Mike. The two officers that were talking to Mike waved to flag it over but the plain clothes officers were already walking over to it. When they finished talking the sector car pulled off and the two plain clothes officers started to walk towards Mike and the two patrolmen.

The patrol officers walked over to Mike and cut the plain clothes officers off from getting close. Then all four started to talk to among themselves; meanwhile Mike rested in the street

THE DAY AFTER LIFE

on his knees by the driver's side of his car. After a few minutes the Patrol Officers walked back over to Mike and stood him. The female officer said, "Look kid this is what we are gonna do. First you should know that those plain clothes officers are no joke, so if what you are saying is true then this is your worse nightmare unfolding. You need to go home, tell your father what happened have him take it from there. Understand that those officers are going to receive and have access to our report on this stop; so your license, name, student status, everything that is in the report will be available to them in the file. In support of that, our dashcam has a video and audio record as well. Now we can't advise you on what to or not to do. We are going to cover our asses and give you a ticket for having an open bottle of alcohol in public it carries a fine of $75. We wish you luck."

Then they took the handcuffs off of him and watched him get in his car and back, back around the corner and then drive off.

Once Mike got back to campus he was so nervous he almost didn't notice the FedEx envelope that was sitting on his front passenger seat. He grabbed it and began to open it as he called his father to tell him what had just happened. By the time he finished talking to his father he had opened the envelope and was about to read its contents. His father told him to take the first plane leaving for their beach house in Puerto Rico and he would contact the Police Commissioner as soon as they hung up. He told Mike to call him when he arrived in Puerto Rico and he would tell him what he found out.

Mike hung up and read the letter inside the FedEx envelope,

THE DAY AFTER LIFE

and when he did he couldn't believe his eyes. He was selected to receive a scholarship for $250,000 as an honorarium for humanitarianism. That was when Mike decided that he would pack and then go stay at his parent's house in Long Beach later that evening, leave to stop and pick up his honorarium in the morning, and then fly out to Puerto Rico the next afternoon.

THE DAY AFTER LIFE

CHAPTER 3

ARRIVAL AT CHARITIES UNLIMITED

THE DIPLOMAT

Harold found himself standing in a rather bland looking conference room. There were no doors, walls or windows yet he knew it was a conference room. The room was bright yet there were no lights or lamps. Then suddenly in walked a tall thin man with a small goatee in a white suit with a white shirt and tie, and white shoes and socks. He was followed by a younger man who seemed to be carrying the older man's briefcase. The younger man was similarly dressed but he had no goatee.

From the other side of the room a man walked in carrying a small white leather looking portfolio. He was wearing a blue suit, white shirt, blue tie, black shoes, and was clean shaven.

Each of the men sat down in a white chair, at the same time; with the first two sitting across the table from the other. No one sat more than four seats away from the single red chair that stood just in front of where Harold was standing.

The first man to arrive, had his young assistant place his briefcase on the conference table, open it, take out a notebook

THE DAY AFTER LIFE

and turn to a specific page. Then he sat it in front of him as if he did not want to touch it. Then the man in blue quietly opened his portfolio and put on his reading glasses and began to read to himself.

The man in white with the goatee nodded at the man in blue as if signaling him to proceed.

But the gentleman in blue continued to review his notes. Then the younger assistant reached in his inside suit jacket pocket and pulled out an envelope and slide it across the table just close enough for it to come to a rest in front of where Harold was still standing behind the red chair. When it came to rest Harold reached and picked it up. It had his name on it so he opened it. At this point no one has said one word.

When Harold opened the letter he saw that there was a bank check in it in the amount of $5 million dollars payable to Cash with his name noted on the memo line. Harold smiled and said, "Thank you." The young man smiled and nodded.

Then the man in blue, with the portfolio spoke and said, "Please make yourself comfortable and have a seat. Mr. Frye or Harold if I may, my name is Louis Fowler and I have a few questions about your intentions concerning the honorarium you just received. If you would now give me your full attention I would appreciate it.

Harold sat down, smiled and said, "Of course."

Then Louis said, "Harold you were born April 21, 1962. You are married to your wife Linda for 30 years. You have three children, Harold Jr., Mark Anthony, and Linda Jr. You live in the East Hampton on Long Island and you work as a Deputy Diplomat at the Office of the United Nations in midtown Manhattan. You recently returned from a diplomatic mission to the Philippines and you have plans to retire later this year or as soon as your son Harold Jr. finishes his studies at your old alma martyr, when he could be considered as your replacement in the diplomatic core. Am I correct so far?"

Harold nodded and said, "Yes all of that is correct. It has been a long standing family tradition that Frye men work in the diplomatic core. We are very proud of Harold Jr. for wanting to follow in the family's tradition of public service."

Louis looked over his reading glasses and said, "Is that so?" Harold taken aback for a moment continued to smile and said, "Yes, Sir. And may I ask why this information is pertinent?"

Louis smiled and said, "No, you may not. We are here to determine the next step for you. You do realize that to one much is given, much is required? We just want to make sure that, you understand what is required of you. And quite frankly Mr. Frye we are very concerned about what you plan to do with our honorarium. Or at least I am. I'll let my colleague across the table make Ns own determination in a moment."

Now a little concerned, Harold responded and said, "I was under the impression that this honorarium was a gift that I might do what I pleased with it. There was no indication that there were any proviso's or stipulations attached to it;

otherwise I might just reconsider my acceptance."

Louis smile and said, "This is exactly why you were selected for such a substantial award sir. It seems that over your life you have always looked out for your best interest first and never the interest of other."

Harold now becoming uncomfortable said, "I take exception to that sir, I have lived a very charitable life and been quite considerate of my fellow man."

Louis smiled and said, "Oh! Really sir? Isn't it true that the only reason you make substantial charitable gifts, specifically to your brother-in-laws homeless shelter and church, is to lower your taxable income? And isn't it true that the men your brother-in-law houses at his shelter are routinely used to maintain your gardens and landscaping as well as provide handy man services around your home?"

Harold now beginning to become very uncomfortable smiled and said, "You have that all wrong, many of the men at my brother-in-laws shelter are required to do community service under their probation arrangements and my brother-in-law has found it difficult to place these people with homeowners who sometimes fear they maybe taken advantage of or even robbed."

Then Louis said, "So let's talk about income tax planning; why is it necessary to write off hotel stays, lavish dinners and gifts for your Chief of Staffs sexual favors? Wouldn't it be more accurate to just name her as a dependent? Or would your wife not

THE DAY AFTER LIFE

approve?"

With that Harold turned beet red but before he could say a word, Louis continued and said, "But let's talk about your retirement plans and your son, Harold Jr. Particularly your hopes of Harold Jr. replacing you in the diplomatic service. Isn't it true that your son has told you on numerous occasions that he wasn't interested in joining the diplomatic core and that you had to pull as many strings as possible to box him into a corner leaving him no other option but to join the Diplomatic core? But before you answer that please enlighten us about your plan to stifle your three year unpaid interns hopes of replacing you in the diplomatic core just so you guarantee there would be an opening for your son?"

Harold now very uncomfortable attempted to address the allegations but he was interrupted by Louis once again.

Louis continued to smile and said, "Hold on, none of that is really relevant for these proceedings. Let's cut to the chase here. Please just tell us why you have done everything in your power to keep the Subic Bay Military installation in the Philippines when you know there is no strategic need for it there and that the people of that country do not want it there. And don't tell us, it is because the President has given you, your matching orders and you are just doing what you were told to do."

Harold sat up and said, "Sir I take exception to this line of questioning. Not one word of any of your allegations is true.

THE DAY AFTER LIFE

And I will not dignify any of them with a response."

After Harold's out burst both Louis and his colleague turned around and faced what seemed to be a wall at the far end of the conference table were suddenly a very large television screen appeared. What appeared on the screen started off as if someone had just loaded a 8 miller media film reel and all of the up front markings had to run through before the show actually started. When it did everyone in the room saw and heard a video of Harold plotting and scheming to do each of the deeds Louis had just accused him of; live and in living color. When the video started to run scenes of Harold and Rita having sex Louis stopped it by saying that is enough.

Harold quietly sat back in his chair and slumped down. Then everyone turned back around and faced him. Louis said, "Let me sum up my case here Mr. Frye. I know that the money Charities Unlimited has honored you with is going to a selfish, bitter small minded man and I have just proven it; just by what you have done in the past."

Louis leaned close to the conference room table and placed his elbows on it in front of him and said, "Isn't it true, that you would rather see the people of the Philippines suffer continued moral decay as present day economic hostages to the drug fueled, sexual depravity of drunken American sailors and other military personnel stationed there, because you are ashamed and bitter about the fact that you have several half brothers and sisters of Pilipino decent. Outcast fathered by your grandfather when he was stationed over there?"

THE DAY AFTER LIFE

The room already silent became as cold as ice for a moment. Harold sat stunned by Louis' statements but there wasn't anything he could say because he knew that Louis was right and he didn't want to see or hear of the scenes from his past concerning statements or thoughts about his siblings in the Philippines. By now Harold was thoroughly embarrassed and ashamed.

Then Louis sat back, closed his portfolio, took a deep breath and said, "May case against Harold Frye is simple. Harold Frye is not representative of those principals and ideals that underpin the spirit and or philosophy that Charities Unlimited has become known for. I say... No; I have proven that Mr. Frye is the epitome of an unforgiving, bitter and angry man, full of hidden resentment and hatred for people." Then Louis sat back in his chair.

Then the young man who carried the briefcase of the man wearing the goatee stood up and said, "Here ye, here ye, here ye Apostle Jeremiah will now begin his query of Harold Frye, everyone come to order and hear what is to be." As soon as he finished he sat back down.

Apostle Jeremiah cleared his throat and said, "I'm not sure if the gentleman on the other side of the table had a chance to set the record straight for this query but let me proceed with my query and we can set the record straight when I have finished. First let me honor the Most High and give thanks for this opportunity to meet you Mr. Frye. My associate and I will attempt to clear up or set the record straight concerning the points that have been

THE DAY AFTER LIFE

leveled against you thus far. Further inquiry into those and other matters may or may not be required of you later."

Harold sat up in his seat in preparation to speak and Apostle Jeremiah looked at him and said, "There is no need to speak right now, there will be plenty of time for that when you are finished here." And although Harold tried and tried to interrupt by speaking he could not utter a word or even make a gesture, so finally he just sat back and quietly listened.

Then Apostle Jeremiah pulled the notebook his assistant had sat before, closer and began to read.

He said, "In the matter of your son, Harold Jr. let the record note that Harold Jr.'s destiny does not rest in his father's efforts or lack thereof. It is noted that Harold Sr. loves his son dearly, even more than life itself and only wants the best for him and his future."

Jeremiah continued and said, "And in the matter of Harold Sr.'s adulterous activities, which have been countless in nature, it should be noted that unbeknownst to him, he is, and I will address this issue further in a moment, under a generational curse. That is, his father and his fore fathers before him were under a family curse that was leveled on their great, great, great, grandfather for sins of the heart he committed before any of the forefathers were conceived. Since Harold Sr. did not know of the curse and did not find himself in a position to know, that would be by attending a Holy Ghost filled Bible based church, that charge can not be attached to him.

THE DAY AFTER LIFE

Now let me move to the single most important concern offered by the gentleman across the table from me, that of 'Unforgiveness, bitterness, anger, resentment, hatred and jealousy for his Philippine American siblings and by extension the Philippine peoples.'

Right here a little background may help. Mr. Frye believes he is a descendent of an African American male and an Asian American woman, and thus has a unique sensitivity and compassion for people of the Asian culture. Thus on the one hand it would seem hypercritical of him to hold any kind of dislike for his Phillippino relatives as well as the Phillippino peoples. However man's heart is a deceitful thing and harbors' sin and evil. What Mr. Frye does not know, even in light of his expensive genealogical certifications, is that he too is of Phillippino decent. Mr. Frye your great, great, great, great grandfather and mother were of pure Phillippino blood, he a prince and she his princess. And through intercultural marriages both Phillippino, white and Black bloodlines are carried in you. This information was not available to your genealogical researchers but our records date back much further and are much more accurate.

But my concern here is not the truth's that you knew or didn't knew. My concern is that you find pleasure in harboring the spirits of resentment, unforgiveness, bitterness, anger and hatred for people. You have a desire to live as if you are better than others. There is where I want to start my query, please respond."

THE DAY AFTER LIFE

Harold took a deep breath and realized that he could now speak so he pondered what he would say for a moment and then said, "Sir! I am not sure who either of you two are, or what this line of questioning has to do with this award. However I am willing to indulge you to a point and right now I have heard quite enough of these insulting and baseless innuendos and falsehoods. Now if either of you have the power to resend this award I beg you do so for I have answered all of the questions I intend to answer for either of you. Good day." And he started to get up to leave.

When he stood up and turned to leave he realized that there was no door behind him, or window; so after turning and looking around a couple of times he finally said, "Where is the exit?"

Apostle Jeremiah smiled and said, "Why don't you return to your seat for a moment and let me explain how this works." Harold reluctantly returned to his seat, sat down and attentively listened.

When Apostle Jeremiah saw that Harold had relaxed and settled down, he turned to the wall, as did Louis and his assistant, where the video screen had appeared earlier. As it seemingly powered up Apostle Jeremiah said, "Let me show you something before we get to the explanation on exiting this discussion. But first this family tree might help to clear up a few things. Notice here that every name listed on this first screen is familiar to you. I'm not going to sit here and name names because I know you know all of the names shown here as well

THE DAY AFTER LIFE

as the faces. This next screen shows you all of those members of your father's generation. Now some of these people you not only don't know but you have never seen before yet I assure you, they are in your bloodline. Now the next four hundred screens chronicle your entire family lineage back to Adam and Eve. Yes that far back, I'm not going to show you the faces or names of who they are or who is to come because there will be plenty of time for you to learn about and to meet them after this.

Oh! Yes. That is right, however the only question that would need to be answered now is from what position will you be learning about and or hearing about or meeting them from?"

Then Apostle Jeremiah turned back to Harold who was sitting in awe as his family lineage flashed across the screen, when he saw the final slide, that of Adam and Eve his mouth dropped on the conference table and as the light blub flickered in between his eyes, Apostle Jeremiah said, "Yes Harold that was Adam and his wife Eve. And yes, you are dead."

Then Harold teetered over in his chair and fell on the conference table face first. After about two or three minutes he regained consciousness and sat back up. And in a low quiet voice Harold said, "I'm dead? When? How? Why me?"

Apostle Jeremiah smiled and said, "All I can say is that God finally found time to meet with you. Right now you are being screened to see if you should meet with him and if so what area or areas you should concentrate on for your meeting with the Most High. It's my century to represent the Lord at the screening table as well as Mr. Fowlers shift to represent the Enemy. Now with that said, "I want to remind you as to where we left off at, in hopes of getting your response before this session expires. Please if you will?"

Harold quietly said, "Would you repeat the question, please, sir?"

Apostle Jeremiah took a deep breath and said, "My question was, do you find pleasure in harboring the spirits of resentment, unforgiveness, bitterness, anger and hatred for people. And do you have a desire to live as if you are better than others?"

Harold didn't say anything at first then he said, "I don't think I should sit here and let either you or him judge me, like this. Do I need a lawyer?"

Apostle Jeremiah looked across the table at John and then at his assistant and then stood up and he and his assistant walked out. John followed them but he never stepped on their side of the room, each left the way they arrived from behind Harold and outside of his view.

Then Harold stood up and again looked for the exit. He thought for a moment and tried to retrace his initial steps into the room but he still could not see the exit that should have been right behind him. So he walked around the conference room table to where the video screen had appeared and he suddenly saw a door with an exit sign over it. Eventhough he realized that it didn't make sense that he could not see the door from where he was sitting he walked over to it anyway.

THE DAY AFTER LIFE

As he reached out to open the handle less door he felt a swift kick in the pants then he realized he was about to drop the tray of food he had in his hands.

Looking confused he turned and looked in the direction of where the kick had to come from, and he looked right into his fathers face, they were almost nose to nose. When he realized who it was he knew exactly what he meant, sense that was the way he normally communicated with him as a teenager.

His father with fire in his eyes, in a strong angry but low voice said, "How many times have I told you to carry the food tray on your shoulder not with your hands in front of you. Now get moving." Harold turned and walked through the swinging doors into the largest dining room he had ever seen. All he could see were tables, customers and waiters as far as the eye could see. He tried to count them but there were just too many of them. As he walked forward into the dining room he noticed a wall of mirrors to his left so he took a look at himself. He had returned to his tall skinny teen self again wearing tight high water black pants, white socks black shoes a white shirt and a black vest. What was shocking about the picture in the mirror was his face, he was no longer the white milk chocolate complexioned long hair teen his father used to kick in the butt to motivate but now he was a dark skinned long haired Pilipino boy. And as he looked into the dining room everyone as far as he could see was light skinned or white skinned.

He looked up and noticed a large table assignment sign all lithe up hanging from the ceiling. On it he saw his name at the

THE DAY AFTER LIFE

bottom. He read the note next to his name and it said, 'Frye--Express lunch tables for today, tables number 640.1 to 3,500.55 now serving table 640.1.

Harold Frye was a 20 plus year Deputy Foreign Diplomat for the U.N. and was on his way home for a long weekend in the Hamptons.

Ambassador Frye had just returned from an extended tour in the Philippine Islands negotiating the expansion of the Subic Bay Pacific Air Base. He and a team of ambassadors had spent several years in laying the ground work to set the islands political leaders in the frame of mind that allowing this expansion would be good for the island's economy eventhough many of the citizenry were against the continued presence of U.S. military personnel. Over the years the populist had begun to blame the U.S. Soldier's for the moral decay of their social and traditional values.

Ambassador Frye had practically been raised to be a part of the diplomatic core, his father and his grandfather were both members of it and he personally believed he was entitled to represent the U.S. interest in the Southwest Asia political arena.

When Ambassador Frye slammed on his brakes a chain reaction was created that feed into Pastor Jackson's destiny. A ruby red 2010 Mercedes 550 convertible driven by NYU Law Student Mike Abraham, which had been waving in and out of traffic since the Whitestone (RFK) Bridge, sometimes at speeds in excess of 85 miles an hour, was forced to jet from the inside lane into the middle lane looking to cross into the outside lane

THE DAY AFTER LIFE

to avoid hitting Fryes Audi.

The first person on the line introduced himself as Mr. Harold Frye a Deputy U.S. Diplomat attached to the U.N. as well as a construction business consultant from Long Island, Riverhead specifically. He openly pointed out that he was there to pick up a substantial honorarium for his philanthropic endeavors. Mr. Frye was a modestly dressed man, wearing a dark blue suite, white shirt and wide yellow tie. He was of mixed decent, a light skinned African American with Asian features. He stood 5' 11" tall and weighed around 175 lbs.

For the first few moments everyone stood quietly not wanting to stir at any one in particular, until finally Marques said, "So; Harold, why do you think you are here?"

Harold said, "Well I have been a member of the Diplomatic Core for over 25 years. I have worked in six different Asian and Southeast Asian countries over that time and I believe I have served this country well. Now, well my award letter did not specify the reason for my honorarium other than to indicate that it was for philanthropic endeavors I would have to agree that over my 25 years in the diplomatic core both myself and my family have done all that we could to be of help to the poor and downtrodden around the world. If I may say so, last year I personally donated over $1 million dollars to various youth organizations right here in upper Manhattan and the lower Bronx."

Marques smiled a big smile and said, "Harold my friend you

forgot something. How much is your award?"

Harold looked around at the faces in the elevator and grind and said, "That question seems a little forward don't you think?" Marques said, "Forward? I thought it more like straight forward but forward does work. So tell us my friend, how much is the award for?" Harold looked around the elevator one more time and said, "This is rather unsettling, a gentlemen never discloses his hire." Marques looked at everyone and said, "Wouldn't you like to know?" Everyone shook their head yes and Marques queried Harold again and this time he said, "Was it for $1 million dollars?" Harold smiled and said, "If a man would give that much away in one year why would he hurry down here to pick up what he would normally just given away? No my good man, query someone else, I will not fall prey to your question. My award is between my benefactor and myself. That is all."

Marques laughed out loud and said in a high squeaky voice, "My award is between my benefactor and myself..." Everyone laughed and Harold thought for a moment and then said, "Well if you must know; I just returned from an extended tour in the Philippines yesterday evening and on my way to our team's debriefing a Federal Express Courier stopped me in the parking garage, of all places and handed me an award letter. At first I thought nothing of it but by the time I had reached the conference room I was compelled to open it. That was actually when I realized it was an award letter and from whom it was from. Upon reading it, and as you already know I personally donate a substantial amount of money each year to the needy, the award was for Philanthropic endeavors in the amount of $5

THE DAY AFTER LIFE

million dollars. I was quit surprised. So I went into the debriefing, which is my duty, and first thing this morning I cleared my calendar and drove right over."

When the elevator stopped Marques smiled and said, "Mr. Frye, Harold Frye, this is your stop are you ready for your new future?" Harold looked at Marques and smiled and said, 'All five million dollars of it" and he proceeded towards the elevator doors as they slowly opened. Harold saw that the hallway he was about to enter into was dark except for a glimmer of a flashing exit sign in the distance. Marques smiled and said, "Do not be afraid, Harold Frye, you are in good hands. The lights are motion sensitive once you step into the hallway and move the lights will come up. Go on man, step lively."

Marques laughed a big laugh and Harold stepped out into the dark hallway as the elevator doors closed behind him. Just before the doors fully closed the hallway lights came up and it was suddenly bright as a summer day on the beach. That was when Harold noticed that the hallway was a lot longer then he had thought. It looked as though the hallway went on for miles and miles in each direction. Suddenly he noticed two doors in front of him: a great Oak door and a great Birch wood door, both standing next to the each other.

On the right was the Great Oak Door which was as smooth as glass with no hardware or handle to open it with. The Great Birch door stood on the left and was beautifully adorn with streaks of gold inlaid braids and a massive door handle made from a single cut diamond.

THE DAY AFTER LIFE

Harold examined both doors closely and then pondered the situation. He wondered why such a great difference between the only two doors in sight. Then he decided to go through the Great Birch door. He just had to feel the touch of the cut diamond handle and since he was about to receive such a substantial honorarium it was only fitting he entered in by way of the door most befitting of his award.

As soon as Harold grabbed the cut diamond door handle his whole life flashed right before his eyes.

Back on the Elevator

When the elevator doors closed behind Harold, Marques turned to the remaining guest's and said, "Did you notice a hint of bitterness in the air?" Each of the passengers looked at each other with a confused look on their faces and nodded no. Then Marques said, "It reminds me of a verse from the book of Ephesians the fourth chapter verses 30 to 34 from the King James Bible: '30 And do not grieve the Holy Spirit of God, by whom you were sealed for the day of redemption. 31 Let all bitterness, wrath, anger, clamor, and evil speaking be put away from you, with all malice. 32 And be kind to one another, tenderhearted, forgiving one another, even as God in Christ forgave you.'" Then he looked around into the faces of each of the remaining passengers smiled and said, "You didn't taste that did you?" Then he laughed a loud laugh and the elevator started to move again.

Back in the Hallway with Harold Frye

THE DAY AFTER LIFE

Harold found himself standing in a rather bland looking conference room. There were no doors, walls or windows yet he knew it was a conference room. The room was bright yet there were no lights or lamps. Then suddenly in walked a tall thin man with a small goatee in a white suit with a white shirt and tie, and white shoes and socks. He was followed by a younger man who seemed to be carrying the older man's briefcase. The younger man was similarly dressed but he had no goatee.

From the other side of the room a man walked in carrying a small white leather looking portfolio. He was wearing a blue suit, white shirt, blue tie, black shoes, and was clean shaven.

Each of the men sat down in a white chair, at the same time; with the first two sitting across the table from the other. No one sat more than four seats away from the single red chair that stood just in front of where Harold was standing.

The first man to arrive, had his young assistant place his briefcase on the conference table, open it, take out a notebook and turn to a specific page. Then he sat it in front of him as if he did not want to touch it. Then the man in blue quietly opened his portfolio and put on his reading glasses and began to read to himself.

The man in white with the goatee nodded at the man in blue as if signaling him to proceed.

But the gentleman in blue continued to review his notes. Then the younger assistant reached in his inside suit jacket pocket and pulled out an envelope and slide it across the table just

THE DAY AFTER LIFE

close enough for it to come to a rest in front of where Harold was still standing behind the red chair. When it came to rest Harold reached and picked it up. It had his name on it so he opened it. At this point no one has said one word.

When Harold opened the letter he saw that there was a bank check in it in the amount of $5 million dollars payable to Cash with his name noted on the memo line. Harold smiled and said, "Thank you." The young man smiled and nodded.

Then the man in blue, with the portfolio spoke and said, "Please make yourself comfortable and have a seat. Mr. Frye or Harold if I may, my name is Louis Fowler and I have a few questions about your intentions concerning the honorarium you just received. If you would now give me your full attention I would appreciate it.

Harold sat down, smiled and said, "Of course."

Then Louis said, "Harold you were born April 21, 1962. You are married to your wife Linda for 30 years. You have three children, Harold Jr., Mark Anthony, and Linda Jr. You live in the East Hampton on Long Island and you work as a Deputy Diplomat at the Office of the United Nations in midtown Manhattan. You recently returned from a diplomatic mission to the Philippines and you have plans to retire later this year or as soon as your son Harold Jr. finishes his studies at your old alma martyr, when he could be considered as your replacement in the diplomatic core. Am I correct so far?"

Harold nodded and said, "Yes all of that is correct. It has been a

THE DAY AFTER LIFE

long standing family tradition that Frye men work in the diplomatic core. We are very proud of Harold Jr. for wanting to follow in the family's tradition of public service."

Louis looked over his reading glasses and said, "Is that so?" Harold taken aback for a moment continued to smile and said, "Yes, Sir. And may I ask why this information is pertinent?"

Louis smiled and said, "No, you may not. We are here to determine the next step for you. You do realize that to one much is given, much is required? We just want to make sure that, you understand what is required of you. And quite frankly Mr. Frye we are very concerned about what you plan to do with our honorarium. Or at least I am. I'll let my colleague across the table make Ns own determination in a moment."

Now a little concerned, Harold responded and said, "I was under the impression that this honorarium was a gift that I might do what I pleased with it. There was no indication that there were any proviso's or stipulations attached to it; otherwise I might just reconsider my acceptance."

Louis smile and said, "This is exactly why you were selected for such a substantial award sir. It seems that over your life you have always looked out for your best interest first and never the interest of other."

Harold now becoming uncomfortable said, "I take exception to that sir, I have lived a very charitable life and been quite considerate of my fellow man."

Louis smiled and said, "Oh! Really sir? Isn't it true that the only reason you make substantial charitable gifts, specifically to your brother-in-laws homeless shelter and church, is to lower your taxable income? And isn't it true that the men your brother-in-law houses at his shelter are routinely used to maintain your gardens and landscaping as well as provide handy man services around your home?"

Harold now beginning to become very uncomfortable smiled and said, "You have that all wrong, many of the men at my brother-in-laws shelter are required to do community service under their probation arrangements and my brother-in-law has found it difficult to place these people with homeowners who sometimes fear they maybe taken advantage of or even robbed."

Then Louis said, "So let's talk about income tax planning; why is it necessary to write off hotel stays, lavish dinners and gifts for your Chief of Staffs sexual favors? Wouldn't it be more accurate to just name her as a dependent? Or would your wife not approve?"

With that Harold turned beet red but before he could say a word, Louis continued and said, "But let's talk about your retirement plans and your son, Harold Jr. Particularly your hopes of Harold Jr. replacing you in the diplomatic service. Isn't it true that your son has told you on numerous occasions that he wasn't interested in joining the diplomatic core and that you had to pull as many strings as possible to box him into a corner leaving him no other option but to join the Diplomatic core? But before you answer that please enlighten us about your plan to stifle your three year unpaid interns hopes of replacing you in the diplomatic core just so you guarantee there would be an opening for your son?"

Harold now very uncomfortable attempted to address the allegations but he was interrupted by Louis once again.

Louis continued to smile and said, "Hold on, none of that is really relevant for these proceedings. Let's cut to the chase here. Please just tell us why you have done everything in your power to keep the Subic Bay Military installation in the Philippines when you know there is no strategic need for it there and that the people of that country do not want it there. And don't tell us, it is because the President has given you, your matching orders and you are just doing what you were told to do."

Harold sat up and said, "Sir I take exception to this line of questioning. Not one word of any of your allegations is true. And I will not dignify any of them with a response."

After Harold's out burst both Louis and his colleague turned around and faced what seemed to be a wall at the far end of the conference table were suddenly a very large television screen appeared. What appeared on the screen started off as if someone had just loaded a 8 miller media film reel and all of the up front markings had to run through before the show actually started. When it did everyone in the room saw and heard a video of Harold plotting and scheming to do each of the deeds Louis had just accused him of; live and in living color. When the video started to run scenes of Harold and Rita having sex Louis

THE DAY AFTER LIFE

stopped it by saying that is enough.

Harold quietly sat back in his chair and slumped down. Then everyone turned back around and faced him. Louis said, "Let me sum up my case here Mr. Frye. I know that the money Charities Unlimited has honored you with is going to a selfish, bitter small minded man and I have just proven it; just by what you have done in the past."

Louis leaned close to the conference room table and placed his elbows on it in front of him and said, "Isn't it true, that you would rather see the people of the Philippines suffer continued moral decay as present day economic hostages to the drug fueled, sexual depravity of drunken American sailors and other military personnel stationed there, because you are ashamed and bitter about the fact that you have several half brothers and sisters of Pilipino decent. Outcast fathered by your grandfather when he was stationed over there?"

The room already silent became as cold as ice for a moment. Harold sat stunned by Louis' statements but there wasn't anything he could say because he knew that Louis was right and he didn't want to see or hear of the scenes from his past concerning statements or thoughts about his siblings in the Philippines. By now Harold was thoroughly embarrassed and ashamed.

Then Louis sat back, closed his portfolio, took a deep breath and said, "May case against Harold Frye is simple. Harold Frye is not representative of those principals and ideals that underpin the spirit and or philosophy that Charities Unlimited has become known for. I say… No; I have proven that Mr. Frye is the epitome of an unforgiving, bitter and angry man, full of hidden resentment and hatred for people." Then Louis sat back in his chair.

Then the young man who carried the briefcase of the man wearing the goatee stood up and said, "Here ye, here ye, here ye Apostle Jeremiah will now begin his query of Harold Frye, everyone come to order and hear what is to be." As soon as he finished he sat back down.

Apostle Jeremiah cleared his throat and said, "I'm not sure if the gentleman on the other side of the table had a chance to set the record straight for this query but let me proceed with my query and we can set the record straight when I have finished. First let me honor the Most High and give thanks for this opportunity to meet you Mr. Frye. My associate and I will attempt to clear up or set the record straight concerning the points that have been leveled against you thus far. Further inquiry into those and other matters may or may not be required of you later."

Harold sat up in his seat in preparation to speak and Apostle Jeremiah looked at him and said, "There is no need to speak right now, there will be plenty of time for that when you are finished here." And although Harold tried and tried to interrupt by speaking he could not utter a word or even make a gesture, so finally he just sat back and quietly listened.

Then Apostle Jeremiah pulled the notebook his assistant had sat before, closer and began to read.

THE DAY AFTER LIFE

He said, "In the matter of your son, Harold Jr. let the record note that Harold Jr.'s destiny does not rest in his father's efforts or lack thereof. It is noted that Harold Sr. loves his son dearly, even more than life itself and only wants the best for him and his future."

Jeremiah continued and said, "And in the matter of Harold Sr.'s adulterous activities, which have been countless in nature, it should be noted that unbeknownst to him, he is, and I will address this issue further in a moment, under a generational curse. That is, his father and his fore fathers before him were under a family curse that was leveled on their great, great, great, grandfather for sins of the heart he committed before any of the forefathers were conceived. Since Harold Sr. did not know of the curse and did not find himself in a position to know, that would be by attending a Holy Ghost filled Bible based church, that charge can not be attached to him.

Now let me move to the single most important concern offered by the gentleman across the table from me, that of 'Unforgiveness, bitterness, anger, resentment, hatred and jealousy for his Philippine American siblings and by extension the Philippine peoples.'

Right here a little background may help. Mr. Frye believes he is a descendent of an African American male and an Asian American woman, and thus has a unique sensitivity and compassion for people of the Asian culture. Thus on the one hand it would seem hypercritical of him to hold any kind of dislike for his Phillippino relatives as well as the Phillippino peoples. However man's heart is a deceitful thing and harbors' sin and evil. What Mr. Frye does not know, even in light of his expensive genealogical certifications, is that he too is of Phillippino decent. Mr. Frye your great, great, great, great grandfather and mother were of pure Phillippino blood, he a prince and she his princess. And through intercultural marriages both Phillippino, white and Black bloodlines are carried in you. This information was not available to your genealogical researchers but our records date back much further and are much more accurate.

But my concern here is not the truth's that you knew or didn't knew. My concern is that you find pleasure in harboring the spirits of resentment, unforgiveness, bitterness, anger and hatred for people. You have a desire to live as if you are better than others. There is where I want to start my query, please respond."

Harold took a deep breath and realized that he could now speak so he pondered what he would say for a moment and then said, "Sir! I am not sure who either of you two are, or what this line of questioning has to do with this award. However I am willing to indulge you to a point and right now I have heard quite enough of these insulting and baseless innuendos and falsehoods. Now if either of you have the power to resend this award I beg you do so for I have answered all of the questions I intend to answer for either of you. Good day." And he started to get up to leave.

When he stood up and turned to leave he realized that there

was no door behind him, or window; so after turning and looking around a couple of times he finally said, "Where is the exit?"

Apostle Jeremiah smiled and said, "Why don't you return to your seat for a moment and let me explain how this works." Harold reluctantly returned to his seat, sat down and attentively listened.

When Apostle Jeremiah saw that Harold had relaxed and settled down, he turned to the wall, as did Louis and his assistant, where the video screen had appeared earlier. As it seemingly powered up Apostle Jeremiah said, "Let me show you something before we get to the explanation on exiting this discussion. But first this family tree might help to clear up a few things. Notice here that every name listed on this first screen is familiar to you. I'm not going to sit here and name names because I know you know all of the names shown here as well as the faces. This next screen shows you all of those members of your father's generation. Now some of these people you not only don't know but you have never seen before yet I assure you, they are in your bloodline. Now the next four hundred screens chronicle your entire family lineage back to Adam and Eve. Yes that far back, I'm not going to show you the faces or names of who they are or who is to come because there will be plenty of time for you to learn about and to meet them after this.

Oh! Yes. That is right, however the only question that would need to be answered now is from what position will you be

THE DAY AFTER LIFE

learning about and or hearing about or meeting them from?"

Then Apostle Jeremiah turned back to Harold who was sitting in awe as his family lineage flashed across the screen, when he saw the final slide, that of Adam and Eve his mouth dropped on the conference table and as the light blub flickered in between his eyes, Apostle Jeremiah said, "Yes Harold that was Adam and his wife Eve. And yes, you are dead."

Then Harold teetered over in his chair and fell on the conference table face first. After about two or three minutes he regained consciousness and sat back up. And in a low quiet voice Harold said, "I'm dead? When? How? Why me?"

Apostle Jeremiah smiled and said, "All I can say is that God finally found time to meet with you. Right now you are being screened to see if you should meet with him and if so what area or areas you should concentrate on for your meeting with the Most High. It's my century to represent the Lord at the screening table as well as Mr. Fowlers shift to represent the Enemy. Now with that said, "I want to remind you as to where we left off at, in hopes of getting your response before this session expires. Please if you will?"

Harold quietly said, "Would you repeat the question, please, sir?"

Apostle Jeremiah took a deep breath and said, "My question was, do you find pleasure in harboring the spirits of resentment, unforgiveness, bitterness, anger and hatred for people. And do you have a desire to live as if you are better than others?"

THE DAY AFTER LIFE

MABLE SHELBORNE

Mable, a forty-two-year old, short, heavy-set black woman was so excited she could hardly speak. She was sweating, and huffing and puffing having run from the bus stop.

Mable Shelburne was a single parent of six children all fathered by different men. She had arrived on the bus. Mable was over weight but had a very happy and joyful personality. Mable smiled and shyly said, in a low, sweet voice, "I won, I mean I have been honored, no I mean God has blessed me to be honored with a $100,000.00 award for 'Volunteer of the Year.'"

The Decision

Mable put her head down and reached to push the great oak door open, but when she touched it her whole life flashed before her-- from birth to the moment Clarice walked out of the apartment, and a tear rolled down her face. When she reached to wipe it she heard what sounded like a great clap of thunder. It was so loud she thought the sky had cracked open, and when she looked up she saw Pastor Thomas standing at the church altar, waiting for her as her father walked her down the aisle towards him. What was so surprising was this time she wasn't standing in the choir box. This time she was the bride. Mable could see all of her children standing beside their fathers along the aisle, and somehow she knew they were all clean, neat, and happy, watching her...

I think that was Mable Shelburne you're talking about-- she was awarded $100,000.00 for 'Volunteer of the Year.' Now, she was

THE DAY AFTER LIFE

living a poor woman's life but she was nice and happy—a God-fearing woman. I know she had made some mistakes in life and made some bad choices, but they were all for good reasons. Those decisions were based on all she knew at the time. Her family had lived under a curse of poverty for generations. Her mother and her grandmother had similar challenges, and although they tried to teach her better, she still fell prey to what was familiar and easy. I know her commitment to the Lord had never wavered but she just couldn't seem to get out of her own way at times. Now, one of her daughters did make it out of that ghetto but that one hurt Mable deeply in the end. I can see it now. It was a deep cutting hurt. The young lady blamed her mother for a life of failure. Now Mable's other daughter has also fallen prey to that same family curse. I know she prayed for her mother's faith to hold out, until her change could come. Now, come on, Rufus, tell me what happened to her."

"I can't tell what I don't see yet, hold on a minute, my friend, here it comes now," Rufus answered. "Okay first when Mable was at the great doors. ... She put her head down and reached to push the great oak door open, but when she touched it her whole life flashed before her-- from birth to the moment Clarice walked out of the apartment, and a tear rolled down her face. When she reached to wipe it she heard what sounded like a great clap of thunder. It was so loud she thought the sky had cracked open and when she looked up she saw Pastor Thomas standing at the church altar waiting for her as her father walked her down the aisle towards him. What was so surprising was this time she wasn't standing in the choir box as usual. This time she was the bride. And while she could see all of her children standing along the aisle, somehow she knew they were all happy, clean, neat and standing with their fathers watching her..." Rufus said. "Now hold on a minute here comes some more: Mable Shelburne: This morning at breakfast when her daughter Clarice walked out of the family apartment, she began to cry out. As she thought about what Clarice said, she became more and more distraught. At one point Mable walked over to the kitchen window, which overlooked the building's entrance, hoping to see Clarice before she left the building. As she leaned out of the third floor window to call to Clarice, a shot rang out from in front of the liquor store across the street, the result of a robbery. Mable was hit dead center in the head and died before she could even call Clarice's name.

PASTOR WILLIE JACKSON

As Pastor Willie Jackson pulled his 1975 white on white Buick Grand Prix onto the Cross Island from the feeder ramp which emptied off of the Grand Central parkway he hesitated just momentarily, maybe a half a second longer then he would normally have done under similar circumstances and conditions. That moment of hesitation resulted in a set of events that would change not only his life but that of three other innocent people and their families forever.

When the elevator stopped again both Marques and Pastor Jackson knew whose stop it was. As the doors opened Pastor Jackson, who was standing in the back of the elevator said, "Well this is my stop, so if there is anything you would like to tell me or say about me before I leave please feel free to do so now."

Marques smiled and said, "I like you. So often this is not the case, when the last guest steps off to their destiny I am left wanting to tell them what has been laid on my heart or spoken to me as I did not do with the earlier guest. Usually I can only comment behind their backs. But you have the courage and conviction of a true man of God and I like that. So without further a due what has dropped in my spirit are the words from Isaiah chapter 9 verses 2 through 6 the King James Version; '2 The people who walked in darkness Have seen a great light; Those who dwelt in the land of the shadow of death, Upon them a light has shined. 3 You have multiplied the nation And increased its joy; They rejoice before You According to the joy of harvest, As men rejoice when they divide the spoil. 4 For You have broken the yoke of his burden And the staff of his shoulder, The rod of his oppressor, As in the day of Midian. 5 For every warrior's sandal from the noisy battle, And garments rolled in blood, Will be used for burning and fuel of fire. 6 For unto us a Child is born, Unto us a Son is given; And the government will be upon His shoulder. And His name will be called Wonderful, Counselor, Mighty God, Everlasting Father, and Prince of Peace.' Those verses rest on the word of harvest. Reaping what you sow, is the point and you my friend will reap what you have sown."

Pastor Jackson smiled and said, "I know that is so true and while I am concerned that I have probably sown a thing or two that I'd rather forget, I receive that prophesy and thank you for your obedience in giving it to me. Now I must depart, goodbye Sir."

THE DAY AFTER LIFE

And Marques responded and said, "Remember my friend the good gardener reaps only the good because he reaps after the separation of the wheat and the tares."

Pastor Jackson thought for a moment and then smiled and stepped off of the elevator in to the darken hallway.

As the elevator doors closed behind him the hallway lights came up quickly and brightly. They revealed the two great doors that stood in front of him. By the time Pastor Jackson's eyes fully adjusted to the bright hallway lights only one door was visible, but somehow he knew there was a second door right next to it. So he reached out and pushed the great Oak door open and stepped inside.

As he crossed the doors threshold his whole life flashed before his eyes and in a split second the memory of him sitting on his bed and crying at the passing of his wife just hit him smack between his eyes.

Pastor Jackson and his wife, First Lady Thelma Jackson had been high school sweethearts and married in their first year of seminary school. Before her death in a tragic drunk driver accident about five years earlier they had been married for almost 40 years. They never had children but they were best friends, confidants and church builders. Eventhough First Lady Jackson never accepted her calling many called them Apostles; but in the Baptist faith the title of Apostle is not well recognized.

That memory of his wife reminded him of his loss and

THE DAY AFTER LIFE

emptiness, so much Pastor Jackson began to cry as he walked into the white on white conference room. When he realized were he was he wiped his eyes and that was when a man dressed in a all red outfit walked in carrying a single white piece of paper.

Pastor Jackson attentively watched the man in his red suit, red shirt, red tie red socks and red shoes, walk right past him and take a seat at the white conference table in one of the nine white chairs. When the man; a clean shaved middle aged distinguished looking gentleman, sat down he pointed to Pastor Jackson and signaled that he should sit in the red chair at the foot of the table.

Pastor Jackson looked at the chair and then back at the man as if to say, here? And the gentleman nodded yes. Then Pastor Jackson walked around the table to the first white chair next to it and sat down. The gentleman spoke and said, "I know you; which is interesting because only a few of the people I see here, I can say that to."

Then in walked two other gentlemen both dressed in all white an elder gentleman who was followed by a younger man. When the two approached the conference table the younger man pulled the second seat next to Pastor Jackson, away so that the elder gentleman could be seated. Then he himself sat in the chair behind the elder gentleman. This resulted in three men seated across the table from the man in red. After he sat down the younger man pulled a small jewelry box from his suit jacket pocket and placed it on the table in front of the elder gentleman. The box was larger than a ring box but smaller than a watch box.

Once the two gentlemen in white had settled into their seats the man in red acknowledged them with a nod; they responded with a nod also and then the gentleman in red turned and started to speak to Pastor Jackson.

The man in red spoke and said, "My name is Lee Johnson." Then he reached in his inside jacket pocket and pulled out an envelope and slid it over to Pastor Jackson. Pastor Jackson picked up the envelope; opened it and saw that it was a bank check made payable to him in the amount of $100,000. Pastor Jackson looked further at the check and noted that it was drawn on the Bank of Heavenly Treasurers and he looked up at Lee Johnson and then over at the two gentlemen in white, smiled and nodded thank you to them. They responded and nodded back. Lee Johnson smiled and nodded but Pastor Jackson did not respond.

Then Lee Johnson smiled again and said, "I know you. But you may not remember me. But for now I have a few questions for you." Pastor Jackson smiled and said, "And I have a few for you too." Lee said, "Unfortunately this is not the forum for an open debate so if you'll be kind enough to hold your questions to such time that it is appropriate I would like to begin."

Pastor Jackson looked at him with a strong determined look and said, "Now I know who you are and I have no plans of reframing from anything and or answering any of your questions."

THE DAY AFTER LIFE

Lee smiled and said, "Are you sure that is your wish?" Pastor Jackson started to speak and then he thought for a moment and finally he sat back in his chair took a deep breath and said nothing.

Then Lee smiled again and said, "I know you. Pastor Willie Jackson, age 65, widowed and in foreclosure. Can you explain what you plan on doing with the award money you just received for Religious Endeavors?"

Pastor Jackson watched Lee very closely but he sat silently.

Then Lee said, "Well while you contemplate that question let me ask you this, tell us about the great pleasure you took when your lies about your best friend Elder Dent culminated in his arrest for identity theft."

Pastor Jackson's maple brown complexion turned beet red but he continued to remain silent.

Then Lee Johnson said, "Maybe that was to long ago for you to remember, so tell us did you enjoy watching your wife suffer before she died from a cancer you inflicted upon her?"

Pastor Jackson deliberately looked around the room as if ignoring the question and remained silent.

Then Lee smiled and said, "Ok I see your strategy here. Let me offer you an additional $100,000 for your answer to this question; Are you happy with your God?"

Pastor Jackson looked at the two gentlemen in white who

remained perfectly still and expressionless and then he looked at Lee but remained silent.

Lee smiled again and said, "How about I up that gift from an additional $100,000 to a cool $1,000,000 for a simple 'Yes or No' answer to any of my questions?"

Pastor Jackson continued to stare at Lee but did not say a word or make a gesture of acknowledgment.

Finally Lee acquiesced and turned to the gentlemen in white and said, "Why don't you try for a while and I'll try again later?"

The younger man nodded and then stood up and said, "Here ye, here ye, here ye the Apostle David is about to speak, let all that have an ear to hear pay attention" then he sat back down.

Apostle David cleared his throat and looked at Pastor Jackson and said, "I too know who you are, but let me put it this why; I know you better than my adversary across the table. Only the Father knows you best and His spirit does rest on you." Pastor Jackson responded and said, "God Bless you Sir. I thank Him for all He has done in and through my life, Bless you."

Then Apostle David said, "For the record why have you not entertained the adversary's representative?" Pastor Jackson said, "They enemy will repay you for what he has stolen seven fold. And I recognized him as he recognized me."

Apostle David smiled and said, "Wisdom has been your portion so why do you doubt?"

THE DAY AFTER LIFE

Pastor Jackson bowed his head and said, "The adversary had whispered in my ear everyday since my wife went home to Glory and it has taken a heavy toll on my spirit."

Apostle David, smiled and said, "You strength may have been tested but you showed yourself mighty each time it was. We saw your conviction shine through your prayers for the saints and the Lord has smiled upon you. That which you received when you sat down earlier is the tip of the balance in your account in heaven. The Father has saw fit that your reward would be greater in your later years than in the former, my son."

Pastor Jackson started to well up, he raised his hands high above his head and said, "Glory to God for the things he has done, glory, glory, glory!"

Then Apostle David slid the small box over to Pastor Jackson and said, "Here is another token, of what the Father has placed in your heavenly account."

Pastor Jackson picked up the small box and before he opened it he said, "Should I wait until I get there before I open this?"

Apostle David looked at him and smiled and then Pastor Jackson opened the box and found a small gold key in it. He pulled it out and said, "Thank you Jesus, thank you Lord, Bless your Holy, holy, holy name."

Then he said, "When will I be able to use this?" Apostle David smiled and said, "You already have, in the spirit but to answer your question I will just say sooner than you think. Just keep it close."

Pastor Jackson unbuttoned his shirt and slipped the key on his gold chain right next to his cross, then closed his shirt back up.

Apostle David looked back over at Lee Johnson and nodded that he was finished.

Lee turned to Pastor Jackson and said, "I have one more question of you and it again only requires a simple 'Yes or No' response. You said, you know me, if you do then call my name?"

Pastor Jackson looked Lee straight in the eye and then looked at Apostle David and the young man seated behind him, and then he sat back in his chair and said nothing.

After a moment Apostle David and his assistant got up and walked out as did Lee Johnson. Pastor Jackson watched the men leave the conference table, walk towards what seemed like a blank wall and then out of nowhere two separate doors appeared and then disappeared. He did note that the door that the Apostle and his aide walked through was a simple large Oak door and Mr. Lee Johnson walked through a large Birch wood door with a cut diamond handle on it. But as soon as he got up to leave the doors were no longer there nor did they reappear. So after standing in front of a blank wall for a few minutes Pastor Jackson decide to try exiting on the other side of the room. When he reached the far edge of the conference table he saw just beyond him an exist sign hanging over an Oak wood door. He cheerfully stepped to it and when he reached for it, it opened and he saw a beautiful gate. Through the gate he could see a great meadow with two large trees in the center with a beautiful bright rainbow stretched above them.

He did not see a latch on the gate or a handle but he did notice his wife standing near one of the trees in the great meadow. His heart fluttered when he saw her and as he waved at her with one hand he reached to still his heart with the other and the gate opened. He ran toward her and when they finally embraced they were one.

MIKE ABRAHAM

The next person on line was a tall thin law student named Mike Abraham. He was studying law at NYU focused on investment and finance law. He too boasted of being the recipient of a large cash award from Charities Unlimited and figured he'd pop in and pick it up before his mid afternoon Marketing class. Mike stood over 6'6" tall and weighed 200 lbs soaking wet. With pale white skin he looked as if he needed a tan. He had dirty blonde hair and thick red lips. He was wearing Bermuda shorts, a polo shirt and flip flops. He carried his car keys and wallet in a pouch rubber banded around his upper arm.

Then Marques turned to Mike Abraham and said, "So Mike tell us your story."

Mike looked around and said, "Listen bro I agree with Mr. Diplomat over there, my award is between me and my benefactor. Can we make this bucket go any faster? I don't want to be late for class?" Marques looked at Mike and said, "Oh! Between you and your benefactor you say. Well that is a good

THE DAY AFTER LIFE

thing, Mike, so tell us what did you get?"

Mike smiled and said, "If I tell you will you hit the overdrive button? Look I had a hell of a day yesterday, and just as it didn't seem it wasn't going to get any better this FedEx guy stopped me in the parking lot and handed me this letter. I thought it was from the motor vehicle so I didn't open it until I got back to the dorm, you know. But I must say I really was surprised when I opened it though, I've heard a lot about this Charities Unlimited, you know. It said, I was selected to receive a $250,000 scholarship award in the category of Humanitarianism. I guess somewhere along the way I did some good that I don't remember, I must have saved someone's virginity or something" and then he laughed out loud although no one else laughed with him.

Back on the elevator

No sooner did Marques stop laughing then the elevator stopped again. This time Marques looked at Mike Abraham and said, "Sir Mike! This is your stop, I believe." The elevator doors opened and the faint sound of rushing water filled the elevator. Mike peered out into the darken hallway and asked, "Are you sure?" Marques said, "Oh! Let me check." Then he looked at his clip board and said, "Oh! Why yes it is. Step lively, please." Mike started to move towards the door and said, "It's dark out there." Marques responded and said, "It is safe, just as I explained to Mr. Frye a moment ago; the lights are motion activated. As soon as you step into the hallway the lights will come up. Now don't tell me a big strong scrapping young man

THE DAY AFTER LIFE

like you is afraid of the dark."

Then Marques smiled a big smile again and said in a loud voice, "Man up and boldly go where your heart desires." Then he laughed a loud laugh again as Mike stepped off of the elevator.

As the elevator doors closed behind him the lights in the hallway quickly came up so bright he had to cover his eyes for a moment so they could adjust to the brightness. Once his eyes did adjust he immediately noticed the two great doors in front of him. Mike was stunned that there were no other doors along the seemingly infinite hallway in either direction.

As he scanned the hallway from end to end he took his eyes off of the great doors in front of him and when he looked back, there was only one door in front of him. Now only the great Birch door with the cut diamond handle was standing before him. Mike quickly grabbed it and pushed it open.

When he stepped forward and saw his whole life streamed before him at lightning speed.

Back on the elevator

Again just as the elevator doors closed behind Mike, Marques looked around at each of the remaining passengers and said, "Did you see that?" Both Judy and Pastor Jackson responded and said, "See what?" Then Marques frowned and said, "It looked like pride was in the atmosphere, you didn't notice it? It reminds me of a verse from the book of James the fourth chapter verses 4 to 8 of the King James version of the Bible: '4 You adulterous people,[a] don't you know that friendship with

THE DAY AFTER LIFE

the world means enmity against God? Therefore, anyone who chooses to be a friend of the world becomes an enemy of God. 5 Or do you think Scripture says without reason that he jealously longs for the spirit he has caused to dwell in us[b]? 6 But he gives us more grace. That is why Scripture says: "God opposes the proud but shows favor to the humble."[c] 7 Submit yourselves, then, to God. Resist the devil, and he will flee from you. 8 Come near to God and he will come near to you. Wash your hands, you sinners, and purify your hearts, you double-minded.'"

Then Marques said, "Maybe its just me this morning?" Pastor Jackson smiled and said, "Ms. Judy it looks like our escort is full of the Holy Spirit this morning, quoting scripture and prophesying. To bad we won't know what he quotes behind us when we leave." And he chuckled when he finished.

Back in the Hallway

Mike stepped through the great Birch door and the glow of the white walls, floor and ceiling kind of stunned him for a second. He had not expected to find himself in such a sterile looking setting. He slowly scanned the room and all he saw was the white conference table, 8 armchairs of which seven were white and the one closes to him was completely red. He stood perfectly still for a moment and then in walked a man dressed in a white three piece suit, wearing a white shirt and tie, white socks and white shoes carrying a black leather looking portfolio. As he laid the portfolio down on the conference table and pulled his chair out to sit he said the Mike, "Please have a seat."

THE DAY AFTER LIFE

Mike said, "Here?" The man said, "Yes, please."

Mike sat down and then in walked two more men. Both dressed in all white but the taller and older looking man had a thick gray beard. The younger man who followed him carried a small brown notebook. The two men approached the conference table and the younger man pulled out the chair for the elder one and placed the small brown notebook in front of him as he sat down. Then the younger man sat next to the elder and acknowledged Mike and the first gentleman that had arrived.

At that point the first gentleman that arrived, turned to Mike, opened his portfolio, pulled out an envelope and slid it over to Mike. Mike picked it up and looked in it. Inside Mike saw that it had a bank check in the amount of $250,000 dollars made out in his name. Mike smiled a big smile, nodded thanks to the men and placed the check inside his wallet.

As soon as Mike settled down the gentleman who had given him the envelope said, "I'd like to begin by marking the record. My name is Theo Edwards and I am here to get an understanding of what we can expect from you now that you have been selected to receive that honorarium for humanitarianism."

Mr. Edwards continued and said, "So let me begin with a couple of basic questions just to set the record straight. Your name is Michael Abraham, you are a law school student at NYU, you live on campus but your permanent residence is with your parents in Long Beach, New York. I assume all of that is true?" Mike acknowledged the question by nodding his head yes.

THE DAY AFTER LIFE

Then Mr. Edwards said, "Now I'll get right to the point; There are no restrictions on how you may use your honorarium however if your car was to no longer be available for whatever reason what kind of car would you replace it and why?"

Mike smiled and said, "Replace the Benz? That is not an option, dude. But for argument sakes I would probably buy another one. I just love the ride and the chicks are drawn to it like a fly to honey."

Then Mr. Edwards smiled a cautious smile and said, "If we were to ask you to limit the usage of your honorarium to only support charitable endeavors would there be any set of circumstances where you would feel compelled not to honor that request?"

Mike smiled and said, "That's a trick question right? You really just want to know if I'd spend the loot on another Benz, right? And then try and argue that no restriction clause, right? Eventhough you verbally suggested that I restrict the use of the funds, right? Well to be honest with you, of course I will honor your request. I respect what you people are doing here and I certainly would not do anything to besmirch your reputation."

"Could we count on you to look after the poor?" Said Mr. Edwards. Mike quickly responded and said, "The poor? Of course! I make it a part of my daily routine to seek out poor people and support them in any way that I can. Why just the other day I gave my lunch sandwich to a poor hunger old lady at the beach."

Mr. Edwards went on and said, "Mr. Abraham would it be safe

to say that our verbal restrictions would or would not hinder you from addressing your personal responsibilities in a timely manner?"

Mike smiled and said, "My personal obligations will always be kept separate and apart from the use of the funds you have given me. I make it a point to keep my personal obligations and responsibilities in order. I would say I stride to be an upstanding citizen at all times in all ways."

"One last question Mr. Abraham, would it be safe to assume that our desire for the usage of the funds in trusted to you will not in anyway conflict with your religious beliefs?"

Mike responded and said, "My religious beliefs provide no restrictions or obligations that would in anyway infringe upon how these funds are to be used."

Mr. Edwards closed his portfolio and turned towards the far end of the conference table, opposite Mike's seat, as did the two other gentlemen seated across from him as a large screen dropped down from the ceiling. A video began to roll and immediately on the screen appeared a replay of the query that had just transpired. But the video showed Mike in a negative light, meaning it was like looking at a live video in a negative format. Mike said, "What are we looking at?" Mr. Edwards turned and said, "We are looking at your spirit's responses to the questions you just answered, kind of a lie detector if you will. Your responses, if honest and correct make you appear in a positive light. However if your responses are deceptive in anyway you will appear in a negative light to the eye, this is quite accurate, I must say."

As the video preceded all Mike could see was himself being portrayed in a negative light; which seemed quite acceptable to Mr. Edwards. When the video finished the screen retracted into the ceiling. Mike said, "That wasn't accurate. I actually meant everything I said. I can't understand why your machine recorded my responses in such a negative light."

Mr. Edwards smiled and said, "Not to worry Mr. Abrahams your responses only confirmed your emotional responses to the questions put forth; here your word is what matters most." Then Mr. Edwards looked over to the other gentlemen at the table and nodded that he was finished.

At that point the younger of the two men stood up and said, "Here ye, here ye, here ye the Apostle Enosh will query the man called Abraham let all come to order and listen" then he sat back down. Apostle Enosh opened the small brown notebook his assistant had laid in front of his and began to read to himself for a moment, then he lifted his head and said, "Mr. Abraham the record has already be set in order by the gentlemen across from me so I will not reiterate that which has already been recorded, however I have one or two questions for you. First; Why do you think you were selected to receive this honorarium and second what did you plan to do with it now that you have it?"

Mike sat up in his chair and said, "Look I don't understand what is going on around here but I'm ready to go. To answer your questions I would say, I intend to spend every dime on my

THE DAY AFTER LIFE

education and all of those things necessary to complete it. If that calls for me to replace my car then I will. More specifically I will if necessary replace my car with the kind of car that makes sense to me. Not you. Now why was I selected? Probably because of my father and his law firm which some day I will be one of the managing partners in, called somebody or some one who wants to impress my father called it in. Now are there any more questions? If not can I go?"

Apostle Enosh smiled and said, "Well I can say for a fact at least you were honest; uninformed, but honest. One final question Mr. Abrahams, I want you to think back to a bright sunny day in 1985. I believe you were 3 years old then. You walked out of your house alone, up the street and crossed a busy 4 lane street winding up in a grassy lot. You were wearing a two gun Lone Ranger holster set. When you realized you were all alone you dropped one of the toy guns and started to cry for your mother who was at home on the porch entertaining a male friend. Do you remember that day?"

Mike said, "I remember that day, but I don't ..." Apostle Enosh interrupted him and said, "...but you don't remember how you got back home or anything else that happened that day, do you?" Mike said, "Yea, that's right, I don't." Then Apostle Enosh said, "Mike you cried out for help, and it came, so why are you having such difficulty agreeing with this request to help others?"

Mike thought and thought and then he dropped his head and said, "That time when I was lost I promised to be a good boy if

THE DAY AFTER LIFE

she would come and get me and when she didn't I promised that if someone would help me find my mommy that I would always be a help to others. I'd forgotten about that promise over the years and now you have reminded me. So; let me say this, I will honor that promise with these funds however I am directed because it still seems as though I am still lost and in need of help."

... Apostle Enosh smiled and looked at Mr. Edwards then back at Mike and said, "I think you got it. Then he and his assistant got up and walked out. Once the two had left Mr. Edwards shook his head and got up and left following the same way he arrived from behind Mike's chair.

When Mike realized all of the men had left and that he did not notice a doorway going in or out, he became concerned. He stood up and looked around the whole room and could not determine how he or the other men had gotten in or out of the room. Then he focused on the area where the video screen had dropped down and walked over in that direction. As soon as he crossed the threshold of the far end of the conference room table, he saw an exit door sign hanging over a door that he did not see earlier.

When Mike reached to push the handle less door it opened and he found himself flat on his back in a hospital bed looking up at the ceiling lamps. He could hear someone say, "...doctor we have a problem, the patient is in cardiac arrest." And it seemed as though all hell broke loose. He could hear people moving, tools dropping, machines beeping and a low constant ringing

THE DAY AFTER LIFE

sound over head. After a few minutes he heard someone say nurse clear and then he could see his body jolt upward. He didn't feel any pain though. This happened two more times and then he heard someone say, "That's it Dr. Ross you've done all you could do, he's gone now." That was when Mike thought maybe they were talking about him and he got scared and tried to speak but no one seemed to hear him. He attempted to wave his arms but couldn't, in his frustration he began to cry and that was when one of the nurses in the room noticed it and passed out. People scrabbled to catch her and revive her, and when she finally pulled herself together she said, "Dr. Ross the patient, the patient, a tear, a tear, he is crying." Mike could see the doctor turn to him and look right into his face; it was if he was looking down drain pipe for a lost ring. So Mike blinked several times as if Morris Code. He blinked a dot, dot, dot, then a dash, dash, dash, and again a dot, dot, dot. When Dr. Ross realized that Mike was using Morris Code he knew Mike was still in there, he immediately conferred with the other doctors and they started to recheck his vital signs and brain waves.

After what seemed like a life time Dr. Ross had Mike moved to another room where they propped him up so he could see better and they attempted more test to see how best to communicate with him.

Finally after days of test Dr. Ross came to Mike and said, "We have done all we can do for you at this point. Until you decide to come back to us, this is pretty much how it is going to be. I've assigned my most trusted nursing team to work with you until you find your way back Mike. I pray you God speed." And he

THE DAY AFTER LIFE

turned and walked away. Mike began to cry, and cry a lot all he could do was shed tears he couldn't holler, he couldn't whimper, he couldn't move, all he thought about was he wanted to come back but he couldn't figure out how to.

They assigned four Black nurses to him and they had to do everything for him. They had to clean him up, feed him through a straw, comb his hair and brush his teeth and turn him over every so many hours. Mike had been paralyzed from the car accident, from the neck down, but he was still alive.

CHAPTER 4

THE QUESTIONAIRE

(Reaping what you sow--short –What have you done for God?)

Would you be shocked to know that when God requires your soul, at that moment of judgment, he reconciles those things you have done here on earth with what he has commanded that we you from Heaven? And in doing so he looks in the Book of Life and reads what it say's. Wouldn't it be interesting if what God was looking at in the Book of Life was similar to an IRS Tax Return?

Which might read as follows:

THE 'I.H.S.' FORM OR THE --IN HIS SERVICE form,

THE HEAVENLY INTERNAL REVENUE SERVICE FORM

For those of us that are still living in the natural world we have no idea of what life will be like when we leave this world and enter the hereafter or the spiritual realm as it is called. However among the things we've all become very familiar with in this natural world is the I.R.S. or the Internal Revenue Service. The IRS is where we annually reconcile our worth, our existence or earnings and wages. That 1040 form that determines the net reconciliation of selected earnings over costs and expenditures to determine what if anything we may owe or are entitled to be reimbursed for, from the general or common good; in

THE DAY AFTER LIFE

connection with the cost of operating our government.

Below we have adopted the IRS 1040 Form for Heavenly purposes. We open with an overview of this adaptation of a IRS Form 1040 as modified for spiritual use as what we call a "I.H.S. Form 1040" or an In His Service form.

Here is what might well be the first page of the I.H.S. form as found in the Book of Life and used by the Heavenly gatekeeper each of us will face when our soul arrives at the Pearly gates.

IHS form Heavenly Entrance Acceptance Form

Let's quickly complete this form for we know not the hour when our soul will be required.

First: Enter Your First Name, Your Last Name, Address, City, State, Zip Code Your Social Security Number and date of birth. Next enter the date you came to Christ and or your Baptism date. Your date of death would be automatically filled in, if this was an actual I.H.S. form.

Next your Filing Status must be determined. Whether you are considered Single, Married, Married Filing Separately, Divorced, or Widowed check the box marked Single, because at this point this is an individual thing.

Exemptions: List each that apply: You-yourself, Spouse, Daughter(s), Son(s), Adopted Children, Abandon Children, Possible Children (see Comments below for more detail) (See Gen. 33:5).

THE DAY AFTER LIFE

Gen 33:5. 5 And he lifted up his eyes, and saw the women and the children; and said who are those with thee? And he said, the children which God hath graciously given thy servant.

Spiritual INCOME SECTION: All of your Spiritual Wages must be entered here. Please include: All amounts YOU contributed to your Heavenly Treasure account (see Matt 6:19-20).

Matt 6:19-20. 19 Lay not up for yourselves treasures upon earth, where moth and rust doth corrupt, and where thieves break through and steal: 20 But lay up for yourselves treasures in heaven, where neither moth nor rust doth corrupt, and where thieves do not break through nor steal:

These include earnings from the times you gave a glass of water to one of God's Prophet's, or a slice of bread to an angel unaware, or a Word of comfort to the brokenhearted or even paid your Tithes (see Definition of Tithes (Lev 27:30-33).

Lev 27:30-33; 30 And all the tithe of the land, whether of the seed of the land, or of the fruit of the tree, is the LORD's: it is holy unto the LORD. 31 And if a man will at all redeem ought of his tithes, he shall add thereto the fifth part thereof. 32 And concerning the tithe of the herd, or of the flock, even of whatsoever passeth under the rod, the tenth shall be holy unto the LORD. 33 He shall not search whether it be good or bad, neither shall he change it: and if he change it at all, then both it and the change thereof shall be holy; it shall not be redeemed.

Add Other Income: Such as Retirement Income, Inheritances, Gifts from Parents, Gifts from Friends, Gifts from Loved Ones

THE DAY AFTER LIFE

and Gifts from Strangers, Gifts from the Church, Gifts from the Saints and Gifts from the Enemy (2 Cor. 11:13-15).

(2 Cor. 11:13-15) 13 For such are false apostles, deceitful workers, transforming themselves into the apostles of Christ. 14 And no marvel; for Satan himself is transformed into an angel of light. 15 Therefore it is no great thing if his ministers also be transformed as the ministers of righteousness; whose end shall be according to their works.

Add Interest Income: Monies gained from the items under Other Income above.

Add Government or Social or Public Income: Welfare, Food Stamps, Social Security, Unemployment, and Student Loans, hand outs, Court Ordered Support, gifts from the church, gifts from Random Saints, Child Support for You or Due to Others in your care or name. Found Money(s), Other Hand outs, Law Suits, Theft of Cash, Theft of Services, Overcharges, Undercharges where you kept the difference (James 5:4).

James 5:4 4 Behold, the hire of the labourers who have reaped down your fields, which is of you kept back by fraud, crieth: and the cries of them which have reaped are entered into the ears of the Lord of Sabaoth.

Add all Winnings from Gambling: Lotto, Dice, Poker, Black Jack, Cee-Low, Su-Su, Bid Whiz, Bingo, Picked Pockets, Bump and Grab, Spades, Checkers, Domino's or other.

Add Self Employment Income: On the Books, Off the Books,

THE DAY AFTER LIFE

Under the Table, Tips and Stiffs.

Add Your Tax Refunds, Other Peoples Refunds you spent or partook of.

Add all Credit Card Advances both Repaid and Still Outstanding.

Add Other Income i.e.: Rental Income, So-Called Consulting Fees, Illegal Commissions, Legal Commissions and Five Finger Discounts (Deu. 24:7):

Deu 24:7 7 If a man be found stealing any of his brethren of the children of Israel, and maketh merchandise of him, or selleth him; then that thief shall die; and thou shalt put evil away from among you.

Calculate the Grand Total Here:

Turn the page over and gather information about what you did with all of that money, funds, wages, gifts, inheritances etc., to determine which gate you will be allowed to enter. If you have a net, positive or credit balance you will be allowed to enter the gates of Heaven and stand for your final interview (You thought it would be that easy?). It is easier for a camel to go through the eye of a needle then for a rich man to enter into heaven. If it is determined that there is a debit balance, a negative balance or even a zero balance you will be immediately dropped into the Pit of Hell. There your destiny has already been determined and no further consideration will be afforded you however your application to enter Heaven will remain on file for a period of 30 centuries in the event Hell actually freezes does over.

THE DAY AFTER LIFE

Proceed!

First: the Standard Deduction, just for your LIFE itself for You, Your Spouse and each of Your Dependents (See dependents Above for full definition). This deduction is literally the cost to God for Keeping you and yours alive for whatever time he did (one second or 120 years...as adjusted).

Then calculate your Comfort Deductions: The cost associated with having clean air, clean water, a place to sleep (regardless of accommodations), the blood running warm in your veins and a sound mind from time to time (You know the times when you didn't lose it and or the Lord had to send someone to help you find it.)

Determine your Itemized Deductions: The cost for Eye sight, for the ability to speak, for the ability to hear, for the ability to touch and for the ability to smell for none of these are required to live life, In His Service; just ask someone who did not have a full portion of one or more of these abilities for whatever reason, birth or accident.

ADD ALL OF YOUR BLESSINGS-These are the things you allowed God to do for others through your being obedient and faithful to him regardless of the cost or inconvenience to you, your life style or your ego.

NOW DEDUCT ALL OF GOD'S BLESSINGS ON YOUR LIFE. These are the things that only God could give you, during your life. The times when he carried you over troubled waters, or carried you through times of great despair, times when life itself was more

THE DAY AFTER LIFE

than you thought you could bare.

ADD EACH TIME YOU CALLED ON HIS NAME TO HELP YOU WITH THINGS YOU NEEDED OR WANTED.

NOW DEDUCT ALL THOSE CALLS THAT HE MADE ON YOUR LIFE AND YOU REFUSED TO ANSWER (This section might take a while to complete).

SUBTOTAL OF ALL OF THE ABOVE CREDITS AND DEBITS AND ADD THEM

TOGETHER HERE:

Subtotal all income on page one. Calculate Obligation or credit or debit balances from each applicable form here and attach the following schedules:

Form(s) 8814b Credit for Recovery from a Physical or Health Problem...i.e.: AIDS, CANCER, BLINDNESS, BAD BACK, and MIGRAIN HEADACHES.

Form 4972 Recovery from Health Problems suffered by a friend or loved one you Prayed for i.e.: Cancer, HIV/AIDS, Poverty, Prison, Abuse, Sexual Abuse or immorality, Alcohol Addiction, Drug Addiction, Evil Spirits, Smoking of cigarettes, or any Spiritual Deliverances and or Healings.

Alternative Debits and Credits:

Attach Form 6251 this is your credit for any 'Souls' you have brought to Christ (see table).

THE DAY AFTER LIFE

Foreign Credit:

Attach Form 1116 as required: Credit for every Praise you sent up that did not have a request attached to it.

Credit for Child and or Dependent Care Expenses:

Attach Form 2441 Credit for every Praise you sent up in support of other Christian's needs (Please remember to double this figure for God honors this).

Education Credits Form 8863:

Add up every hour spent reading and or studying The BIBLE (His Word) on your own time.

Charitable Gifts Credit:

Add up and then deduct the total of all Charitable dollars you put into Church Offering here.

Add all SEEDS SOW and place them here.

Heavenly Retirement Savings Contributions Credit:

Attach Form 8880. Here make the following calculation:

Add UP all Tithes Paid in column (A). Then add up all of your earnings —use the Total on the bottom of page 1 (your Grand Total of Income including your Tithes and place this figure in column (B). Then add the two columns (A) and (B) together and divide by 10%. Take this number and place it in column (D).

Add up the results of Page 2 below. Then take the number of

THE DAY AFTER LIFE

hours you lived and place them in column (E). Multiple that number by 10% and place that number in column (F).

Take the number from the Grand Total on the bottom of page 1 and place that in column (G). Then take the number in column (G) and divide it by the number in columns (E) and (G). This will give you the value of the hours you should have spent servicing the Lord, or Your reasonable service.

ADD: Standard deductions, Comfort Deductions, Itemized Deductions, and Your Blessings. Then Deduct God's Blessings. Add the cost of your needs and wants. Then Deduct all of His unanswered calls. Then see tables for Recovery of Blessings (both yours and loved ones).

Alternative Deductions which include Praise credits, Child and dependent care credits, Education credits, Charitable Gifts credits, Retirement savings credits are now summed up and then adjusted for Total Tithing.

TOTAL THIS PAGE HERE:

THEN TAKE THE GRAND TOTAL ON PAGE 1, DEDUCT ALL ADJUSTMENT

SUBTOTAL AND RECONCIL THEM ON PAGE 3

While God is a just God and a forgiving God we must be willing to REPENT for our Sins. God's attitude on SIN can be found on Form 1 (Ex. 32:34, Is. 44:22, and Ex. 34:7). For those who need a detailed explanation please see 2 Cor. 5:21.

THE DAY AFTER LIFE

Ex. 32:34 34 Therefore now go, lead the people unto the place of which I have spoken unto thee: behold, mine Angel shall go before thee: nevertheless in the day when I visit I will visit their sin upon them.

Is. 44:22, 22 I have blotted out, as a thick cloud, thy transgressions, and, as a cloud, thy sins: return unto me; for I have redeemed thee.

Ex. 34:7. 5 And he lifted up his eyes, and saw the women and the children; and said, Who are those with thee? And he said, The children which God hath graciously given thy servant.

2 Cor. 5:21. 21 For he hath made him to be sin for us, who knew no sin; that we might be made the righteousness of God in him.

Repentance is a request made daily because no man knows the hour when the Lord will return or require thy Soul. And no man knows the hour when he will pass. So we should always Pray and ask for forgiveness and repent from our sins. (see Acts 8:22, Acts 9:1-20, Matt 3:8).

Acts 8:22, 22 Repent therefore of this thy wickedness, and pray God, if perhaps the thought of thine heart may be forgiven thee.

Acts 9:1-20, 5 And he said, Who art thou, Lord? And the Lord said, I am Jesus whom thou persecutest: it is hard for thee to kick against the pricks….

Matt 3:8 8 Bring forth therefore fruits meet for repentance:

THE DAY AFTER LIFE

With that said, need I remind you that at this very moment the opportunity for Repentance may have just slipped away one minute before this thought crosses your mind: now that you are actually at the Pearly Gates-(1 John 1:7, 9). Please be advised that had you referred to Ps. 51:3, 4 and Heb. 12:4 or Ps. 19:13 we would not have had to prepare this form at all.

1 John 1:7, 9 7 But if we walk in the light, as he is in the light, we have fellowship one with another, and the blood of Jesus Christ his Son cleanseth us from all sin. 9 If we confess our sins, he is faithful and just to forgive us our sins, and to cleanse us from all unrighteousness.

Ps. 51:3, 4. 3 For I acknowledge my transgressions: and my sin is ever before me.

4 Against thee, thee only, have I sinned, and done this evil in thy sight: that thou mightest be justified when thou speakest, and be clear when thou judgest.

Heb. 12:4 4 Ye have not yet resisted unto blood, striving against sin.

Ps. 19:13. 13 Keep back thy servant also from presumptuous sins; let them not have dominion over me: then shall I be upright, and I shall be innocent from the great transgression.

Let's finalize this I.H.S. form by determining our SIN balance and then deducting that balance from our overall ADJUSTED SPIRITUAL INCOME (see pages 1 and 2).

First determine the sources of your SINs (SATAN John 8:44),

THE DAY AFTER LIFE

Your Heart (Matt. 15: 19, 20) Natural Birth (Ps. 51:5).

John 8:44. 44 Ye are of your father the devil, and the lusts of your father ye will do. He was a murderer from the beginning, and abode not in the truth, because there is no truth in him. When he speaketh a lie, he speaketh of his own: for he is a liar, and the father of it.

Matt. 15: 19, 20. 19 For out of the heart proceed evil thoughts, murders, adulteries, fornications, thefts, false witness, blasphemies: 20 These are the things which defile a man: but to eat with unwashen hands defileth not a man.

 Ps. 51:5. 5 Behold, I was shapen in iniquity; and in sin did my mother conceive me.

Please list the SINs you have committed: Personal on form 2011 (Josh 7:20), Secret on form 1910 (Ps. 90:8), Shameful on form 1810 (Is. 3:9), Youthful on form 1610 a credit (Ps. 25:7) and Unforgiveable Sin form 2 (Matt. 12:21, 32 and John 8:24) and then deduct any credit earned for Sins of Ignorance form 3 (Lev. 4:2).

Josh 7:20. 20 And Achan answered Joshua, and said, Indeed I have sinned against the LORD God of Israel, and thus and thus have I done:

Ps. 90:8. 8 Thou hast set our iniquities before thee, our secret sins in the light of thy countenance.

 Is. 3:9. 9 The shew of their countenance doth witness against them; and they declare their sin as Sodom, they hide it not.

THE DAY AFTER LIFE

Woe unto their soul! for they have rewarded evil unto themselves.

 Ps. 25:7. 7 Remember not the sins of my youth, nor my transgressions: according to thy mercy remember thou me for thy goodness' sake, O LORD.

Matt. 12:21, 32. 21 And in his name shall the Gentiles trust. 32 And whosoever speaketh a word against the Son of man, it shall be forgiven him: but whosoever speaketh against the Holy Ghost, it shall not be forgiven him, neither in this world, neither in the world to come.

 John 8:24. 24 I said therefore unto you, that ye shall die in your sins: for if ye believe not that I am he, ye shall die in your sins.

Lev. 4:2. 2 Speak unto the children of Israel, saying, If a soul shall sin through ignorance against any of the commandments of the LORD concerning things which ought not to be done, and shall do against any of them:

Each SIN is worth one demerit or one deduction. The good news is every SIN committed counts as one demerit, the bad news is all SINS whether in word, deed or thought are counted whether you initiated it or it rubbed off on you...

NOW YOU ARE READY FOR THE FINAL CALCULATION:

Take the Grand Total from page 1 and deduct all of the debits and credits determined on page 2 including all attachments and determine your net Heavenly Treasure balance.

THE DAY AFTER LIFE

Then add up all of the SIN demerits determined above.

Subtract the Net Heavenly Treasure Balance from pages 1 and 2, from the SIN balance determined above and if you have at least a Net HEAVENLY TREASURE

BALANCE of 1, YOU MADE IT...IF NOT...

THE DAY AFTER LIFE

CHAPTER 5

THE DIPLOMAT

HAROLD FRYE

Lobby Registration Desk

...Rufus turned the volume on the computer speakers slightly higher and they listened to 'Harold Frye quietly say, "Would you repeat the question, please, sir?" Then Apostle Jeremiah took a deep breath and said, "My question was, do you find pleasure in harboring the spirits of resentment, unforgiveness, bitterness, anger and hatred for people. And do you have a desire to live as if you are better than others?"

Harold didn't say anything at first then he said, "I don't think I should sit here and let either you or him judge me, like this. Do I need a lawyer?"

Standing behind Rufus Marques whispered into and said, "Isaiah 55 verses 6 to 9 of the King James Bible say's "6 Seek the LORD while He may be found, Call upon Him while He is near. 7 Let the wicked forsake his way, And the unrighteous man his thoughts; Let him return to the LORD, And He will have mercy on him; And to our God, For He will abundantly pardon. 8 "For My thoughts are not your thoughts, Nor are your ways My ways," says the LORD. 9 "For as the heavens are higher than the earth, So are My ways higher than your ways, And My thoughts

THE DAY AFTER LIFE

than your thoughts."

Rufus responded and said, "Hold on there, looks like something is about to happen and I bet it's not going to go well for this guy Frye."

Then Apostle Jeremiah looked across the table at John, then at his assistant and finally both he and his assistant stood up and walked out. John followed them but he never set foot on the other side of the room where Apostle Jeremiah and his assistant walked. Each walked out the same way they arrived, from behind Harold and then outside of his view.

Finally Harold stood up and again looked for the exit. He thought for a moment and tried to retrace his initial steps into the room but he still could not see the exit that should have been right behind him. So he turned back and walked around the conference room table to where the video screen had appeared and he suddenly saw a door with an exit sign over it. Eventhough he realized that it didn't make sense that he could not see that same door from where he was sitting at the conference table, he walked over to it anyway.

... As he reached out to open the, handle less, door he felt a swift kick in the pants. That was when he realized he was about to drop the tray of food he had in his hands.

Confused he turned and looked in the direction of where the kick had come from; and he found himself looking right into his fathers face; they were literally, nose to nose. When Frye realized who it was that kicked him, he knew exactly what it meant; sense that was the way his father normally communicated with him as a teenager.

Young Frye's father, with fire in his eyes, in a strong angry but low voice said, "How many times have I told you to carry the food tray on your shoulder not with your hands in front of you. Now get moving." Harold turned and walked through the swinging doors into the largest dining room he had ever seen. All he could see were tables, customers and waiters as far as the eye could see. He tried to count them but there were just too many of them. As he walked forward into the dining room he noticed a wall of mirrors to his left so he took a look at himself. He could see that he had returned to his tall skinny teenage self again, wearing tight high water black pants, white socks black shoes a white shirt and a black vest. What was most shocking about that picture in the mirror was his face; he was no longer the white milk chocolate complexioned long hair teen his father used to kick in the butt to motivate but now he was a dark skinned long haired Pilipino boy. And as he looked into the dining room everyone as far as he could see was light skinned or white skinned Philippino.

Then he looked up and noticed a large table assignment sign all lithe up hanging from the ceiling. On it he saw his name at the bottom. He read the note next to his name and it said, 'Frye-- Express lunch tables for today, table numbers 640.1 to 3,500.55 now serving table 640.1.

Rufus listened and then looked at the sign Harold was looking at on the computer screen and busted out laughing. Marques tried to hold back his laughter but couldn't hold it very long and he too busted out laughing and said, "Now that's a life long job, everyday he's got what over two thousand tables during the lunch rush or he's gonna get a swift, I mean swift kick in the rear. My God what kind of hell is that?"

Rufus said, "I don't know but it looks like he'll be easily recognized among all of his customers. I hope he gets good tips."

STANDING OUTSIDE THE THRONE ROOM

Standing just outside the Heavenly throne room which was so vast even the mind of a mere man could not grasp the magnitude or the majesty of it. The throne room was so great the whole mind of a man could only take in enough to conceive the place that he stood. It was so vast that it requires a full step forward to grasp the understanding of the next inch of sight as it is revealed to you.

As Harold Frye opened his eyes from his nightmarish existence, an eternity of serving in his fathers restaurant, it was all he do to wrap his mind around the feeling that he was now standing in the center of the heart of the universe waiting for something. What he didn't know.

It was clear what his life was like moments before he arrived here: Harold's could not tell one day from another because he never saw the light of day. All he knew was he was seemed to work all day every day serving meal's to people who could not ever seem to be satisfied. Hour after hour, tray after tray and

THE DAY AFTER LIFE

order after order no tips, not even a thank you; just get me this, you forgot that and where is my...

As he pulled himself together he realized he was now sitting inside a court room, a very large court room, with the biggest judge's bench he could have ever imagined. Simple in yet elegantly made. To the right facing the judge's bench seated at his table, was a tall very pale looking man in a black suit, black shirt, black tie wearing black shoes and socks. The man was clean shaved and had a slight order of cigar smoke on his sleeves.

To his left was an elderly man of color, wearing a long white robe ad the longest full gray beard he had ever seen was seated at the table adjacent to his. The only odd thing abut him is that he had no smell, no cologne, no deodorant fragrance, no soap smell, just a feeling, not the actual smell, of a fresh meadow breeze about him.

Both of the gentlemen surrounding Harold seemed to be waiting for something to happen but he did not have a clue as to what was going to happen next. As his eye's wondered around the great room and returned to the magnificent bench in front of him he saw a mature looking man also in a white on white robe standing in front of the great bench. It seemed as if he was in deep thought for what seemed an eternity and then when he finally turned around to face the table Harold and the others were seated at you could see the look of despair on his face. With that Harold noticed a smirk overtake the gentlemen to his right, face and a shared sense of sorrow on the face of the

THE DAY AFTER LIFE

gentlemen seated to his left.

All of a sudden the court room filled with onlookers, dressed in a rainbow of colored robes, some with jewel encrusted crowns and others with simple with of colored turbans. They all seemed to file in quietly which was amazing within itself sense there was so many of them entering and yet you could hear a pin drop as they did.

Once everyone was settled, which seem to happen in a flash the gentlemen standing in front of the judge's bench spoke and said, "What say you adversary?" And the gentlemen seated to Harold's right stood up and began to speak.

THE CASE AGAINST HAROLD FRYE

The Adversary said, "For the record I want to state that against the advice of Counsel Mr. Frye has requested to appeal his case. While his request, as are many others are still pending the formal Event of the Rapture the Adversary welcomes any opportunity to offer up both valid and questionable appeals as they are presented. With that said, I want to report that since Mr. Frye was assigned to our care he has, as is the custom and our charge suffered tremendously, almost unto death. A fitting punishment for the charges that got him assigned to Under-Heaven in the first place."

Before Harold could complete his thought to base a respond on his Counsel continued and said, "The three charges leveled against my client are as follows: First; being a man of privilege and position he lead a protected life. His family, associates, community and even his neighbors quite often went out of their way to afford him every possible comfort and opportunity. I say that because that was the pedestal which was his plight. Yes, with that layer of comfort and protection there was little opportunity for him to find time to, as you put it, suffer. Additionally my client, while fortified by this layer of protectors was never compelled to deter from his regular moral routine thus he never found motivation, as you would call it, to answer any calls or tugs on his heart to do anything other than that which pleased him. And before you to respond, I must say, the father that you entrusted him while he tried his best to modify or re-educate, if you will, this behavior; things like swift kicks in the pants were more like de-motivators rather than motivators. So to conclude our opening statement concerning my client's inability to demonstrate compassion for others, it really wasn't his fault that he was born into a life of privilege that lacked concern for others, because you born him into that situation before time was known. Thus any desire not to make a sacrifice in any way shape or form I submit was not his fault but more so his choice."

He continued and said, "The second charge against my client stems from his inability to respond in the affirmative when asked 'What has he done in your name?' His defense can be gleamed from the above statement. He was given a life of privilege by you and rarely found it necessary to suffer for in your name or for your sake, quite frankly. His family was well provided for, and him by extension. If not for recent events I would have to say; if not for your placing him in this situation, for the first time things were quite different. Let me clarify that

THE DAY AFTER LIFE

point, the death of his Chief of Staff, untimely as it were and certainly not his fault placed him in a very uncomfortable position. If not for his alibi he might have found himself in a position that would have required him to come to you directly for help fostering the kind of circumstances that might have resulted on him effectively demonstrating some suffrage for your names sake. Again a situation that he himself had no direct control over; even if he had a heart, mind or desire to do so."

At this point Harold could hardly contain himself and he started to stand up and take over the presentation of his case. While he still didn't fully grasp the proceedings he realized that the case as presented by his counsel was certainly not in the least designed to help him. But as had happened in the past, no matter how hard he tried he could not open his mouth in his defense and he certainly could not rise from his seat. In his frustration he began to weep.

I close with my clients response to the third and final charge, that of his heavenly inheritance or forfeiture of same. As he is accused of forfeiting his heavenly inheritance due to a lack of efforts, events, activities that go to building one; I refer to your form I.H.S. We understand that after a careful review of this form preparation my client had a debit balance. In other words when comparing all of his earthly activities which would cause him to build up a credit balance in his heavenly account when offset by those activities, efforts and events that would cause a reduction in that same account resulted in a Sin Balance or deficient balance requiring his soul to be forfeited into the hands of Under heaven.

The Adversary rest his case on this single item. We offer that Mr. Frye in addition to our first point; Thus any desire not to make a sacrifice in any way shape or form I submitted earlier was not his fault but more so his choice."Secondly; you directly fostered the circumstances that resulted in my clients effectively demonstrating no desire or willingness to participate in or show suffrage for your names sake; as his life did not afford him direct control over it; or even a heart, mind or desire to do so. And lastly his earthly activities or lack there of which caused him not to build up a credit balance in his I.H.S. account which resulted in a net Sin Balance requiring his soul to be forfeited into the hands of the Under Heaven. And with that the prosecution rest."

THE CASE FOR HAROLD FRYE

Before Harold could speak the elderly gentlemen seated on his left stood up and all eyes turned towards him as he started to speak. The first thing he said, "Glory to the Father, the Son and the Holy Spirit, Bless you for you are worthy." Then he looked out the side of his eye at the gentlemen who represented Harold and began his presentation. He said; "If it pleases the Lord Almighty 'The Prophet Moses' will address the Adversary's challenge towards the Promise of Salvation to the accused, before thy Judgment is rendered as a matter of order ad decency in the matter of the Adversary vs. Harold Frye the case for The Captivity of Harold Frye's soul."

The Prophet Moses continued and said, "Lord I must confess

THE DAY AFTER LIFE

that everything the Adversary has presented is true not only on the surface but to its core. Only you know this man Harold Frye's heart and why he has done what he has or has not done over his life. The accounting is in and the findings as reported on his I.H.S. form are clear and true Lord. And with that as the most compelling piece of the Adversary's case I will start and end my redress there."

"It is true that Mr. Frye was born into a life of wealth and luxury. And yes it is also true that between Mr. Frye's immediate family, friends, relatives, associates and co-workers he has wanted for nothing. Lastly it is just as true that Mr. Frye has never gone out of his way for anyone or for any reason other than a self-serving one. As we prose his I.H.S. form we can quickly see that in all categories of giving he has never participated. Even during those times he found himself in the mitts of the church there was no response to the Holy Spirit's unction to give."

"Both his and his families preoccupation with saving cash on hand and tax planning was so well embedded that you might think the phrase 'charitable giving' meant not unless there is a tax break associated with it."

"Lord as has been your command since the giving of the 'New Testament Covenant of Salvation' that all who ask for it, it shall be given. Let the record show the day Mr. Harold Frye acknowledged his desire to come to Christ and recognize his request."

At that moment just over the heads of all those in the court

THE DAY AFTER LIFE

room a massive bubble appeared with a 3 dimensional surround sound virtual DVD video of a young Harold Frye praying at his bedside acknowledging Christ as his savory and seeking salvation. The virtual memory lasted about 10 seconds and then it disappeared just as quickly as it appeared.

When the video stopped The Prophet Moses continued and said, "Lord, My God, the case against Mr. Frye is strong. It is clear that since that faithful request he has done everything in his human power to draw nearer to you, your ways and even to do your will. Yet you know his heart, you know his story from the beginning to the end. Clearly there is no measure to determine which Sin is greater than another and each Sin is as evil as the other; and no he never made an effort to thank you even for the breath in his body or the wonderful life you gave. I can truly say of all those who have come before him that this is a rare case when there is no evidence of faith, or repentance for the life one had lived. Not even a thank you to a servant or a waiter or a handyman for services rendered has ever been uttered from this man's mouth. The phrase 'I love you' has never been mentioned or even considered during his walk through life. Yes, Lord this is a unique case, but my mission is clear, he asked for salvation thus he may have never done anything to deserve it or earn it he is still entitled to it as you commanded in your Word, my Lord" then he bowed low and sat down in his seat.

Then the Lord turned to the bench and bowed low and with his hands raised high above his head he began to pray, first thanking God the Father for all He has done, then thanking Him

THE DAY AFTER LIFE

for His Word and then making the request for the salvation of Harold Frye without uttering a word himself.

After a moment, that seemed to be an eternity to Harold Frye turned to look at each men, as both the Adversary and the Prophet Moses stood up in anticipation of the Judgment; Harold realized that he was no longer stuck in his chair so he rose as well...

THE DAY AFTER LIFE

CHAPTER 6

MABLE SHELBORNE

Mable put her head down and reached to push the great oak door open, but when she touched it her whole life flashed before her-- from birth to the moment Clarice walked out of the apartment, and a tear rolled down her face. When she reached to wipe it she heard what sounded like a great clap of thunder. It was so loud she thought the sky had cracked open, and when she looked up she saw Pastor Thomas standing at the church altar, waiting for her as her father walked her down the aisle towards him. What was so surprising was this time she wasn't standing in the choir box. This time she was the bride. Mable could see all of her children standing beside their fathers along the aisle, and somehow she knew they were all clean, neat, and happy, watching her...

In the weeks that lead up to the birth of Clarice's son, Zaione Mable had been in good especially good spirit eventhough the cancer in her bones was quickly eating away the time she had left. Every morning Mable get up early and go into the basement bathroom, light a candle and spend upwards of an hour just praying and single to herself. She made it her commitment to pray for each and everyone of her children and her husband come rain or shine. Sometimes the prayers would be for special things that she believed they wanted and other times it would be a general prayer of good health and blessings

THE DAY AFTER LIFE

begging the Lord to have his way in their lives.

Things had been better for her since she married Pastor Thomas eventhough Shay and his the Pastors son did not marry the two raised their daughter Ruth to be a strong and independent young woman and the families, Mables family that is, first college graduate of her generations. Her aunt Clarice was the first college graduate in the family ever.

The delight of Mables heart was the pending birth of Clarices first child. Now at age 35, married, a professional woman at that with a big house out on the south end of Long Island. A successful college educated husband, life for Clarice was picture perfect compared to what she came from.

Some 15 years after Mables wedding to church Pastor Thomas Mable was able to see all of her children except Clarice grown, working, married, with children; and Clarice was about the complete that picture with the birth of her first child, a son.

As for Mable her health problems were more manageable then the sorrow she lived with before her wedding to the Pastor all though things had not always been easy they were much better then they were before the marriage. Mable can look back now and see how her life before the wedding was so how she could not believe that she actually got out of bed some mornings and made it through the day but she thanked God everyday for something no matter how bad things got.

On the morning of her homegoing Mable got up with no more pain than usual, made Pastors breakfast eventhough he had

THE DAY AFTER LIFE

planned to take her for breakfast before he left for the annual men's retreat and golf outing. Mable opted to spend those few minutes with him just sitting on the back porch drinking coffee and eating biscuits with gravy his favorite.

As they sat and reminisce about their life together and the upcoming addition to the family she was able to mask the pain that was deep down in her bones. Somehow Pastor knew something was wrong but she would not admit it and keep it hidden from him. At one moment she grimaced and he had finally had enough and said, "I know there is something wrong and if you don't tell me I am going to make you go to the doctor if I have to drag you." Mable looked at him with fear in her eyes, because he had never made any threatening comments to her before. Like usual she smiled and giggled and said, "I got gas and I was trying to hold it, I'm sorry." They both stirred at each other for a moment and then they broke out laughing but during the moment of laughter Mable yelled out in pain and Pastor Thomas stood straight up and called into the house for help. As he helped her up from the table and into the kitchen Shay came in and asked what was wrong. Mable tried as hard as she could to pass it off as the Pastor was over reacting but he even she could see the pain her mother was in; then Mable collapsed and every one went into panic mode.

By the time Pastor, Mable, Shay and Minister Thomas got to the hospital emergency room Clarice and her husband were on their way from Amityville in Suffolk County driving as fast as they could even in her state of expectancy. Their baby was due any

THE DAY AFTER LIFE

day then.

Pastor Thomas walked down the hall from the Emergency Room registration desk along side the gurney that Mable was being rushed into the emergency room in. As he did he looked into her eyes and said, "Hold on, God will work this out, we'll be right here in prayer until you come out. Love you." Peering back at him through the oxygen mask the doctors had placed over her nose and mouth, all she could was smile and nod her head in agreement.

Just as he turned to walk back towards the waiting room he could see Clarice being seated in a wheel chair and pushed towards the paternity room with his son following close behind the attendants.

The next thing Mable knew she was looking in the eyes of her newest grandson, Joshua. As she marveled at his fragileness she could clearly see the wonderful things he was going to accomplish in his life. Her heart seemed to skip a beat as she felt the love in her pour out over him. And in a blink of her eye she was standing outside the great throne room.

THE CASE AGAINST MABLE SHELBORNE

Almost in a state of shock and bewilderment the harsh reality of where she was and why just washed over her in a flash as she was ushered to her seat at the table sat in front of the throne of grace and judgment. Next to her, on the left, was a beautiful Egyptian looking woman all dressed in a long ruby red gown with one large bright red ruby pendent in her long wavy black

THE DAY AFTER LIFE

hair; her lips were so red they seemed like they were on fire and she smelt of roasted roses Mable remembered thinking.

 To her left was a beautiful dark haired young Jewish woman dressed in a long white on white robe.

Before Mable could say a word or even ask a question the woman in red stood up and as she looked towards the great throne in front of her Mable realized who was standing in between the throne and the table she was seated at.

She was frozen with fear and paralyzed with awe to know that she finally did get to see Jesus, if only for a moment.

The woman in red starred directly a head at the foot of the throne with her head slightly bowed and said in a very surly, yet professional sounding voice, "The Adversary is ready to proceed."

Jesus looked at her as if right through and said, "Proceed with caution." She bowed lower and said, "Excuse." Jesus nodded and she began to speak and said, "The Soul, Mrs. Mable Thomas, First Lady of Bethel Baptist Church and Deliverance Center, is seeking eternal life under the Promise of Salvation and the Adversary objects. I Jezebel speak for the Adversary. I have three points to make and I will not be before you long."

She took what seemed to be a deep breath and below a stream of smoke which revealed a vision for all in attendance to see. A vision of Mable's life flashed in what seemed slow yet hyper motion with in the belly of the smoke stream.

THE DAY AFTER LIFE

The woman in white rose and said, "My Lord is it necessary that counsel proceed with her version of the Soul's life and not yours, as you were with her?"

Jesus nodded and raised his right hand just slightly and Jezebel's smoke screen disappeared faster than it appeared.

Jezebel bowed her head to Jesus and said, "Excuse me." Jesus looked at her and said, "You may proceed again, with caution."

Jezebel bowed low and when she arose this time she bellowed her first charge, which shuck the chair Mable sat in. She said, "Whoredom. Whoredom is the first charge we present. This soul was captive to the spirit of whoredom every day of her life up until you intervened and showed her mercy. The Adversary charges that had you not intervene this soul was destined for the Under heaven. The Adversary asks that for the record, the soul's entire life of whoredom be displayed for all to see."

The woman in white rose and again and said, "My Lord there is no need to record this soul's life as defense counsel will stipulate to the grounds for the charge and as it is true, you were with the soul everyday, so you know first hand what this soul did or didn't do."

Jesus looked at the woman in red, who had already bowed even lower than she had done earlier, and he said, "The objection is so stipulated, proceed."

Jezebel stood up and as she straighten the ruby in her hair she said, "The Adversary charges this soul with a lack of faith as well. Time and time again this soul, even in your presence Son of Man, cried out and demanded relief from her financial situation while all along not adhering to your principal of tithing. And to make matters worse she selfishly begged for mercy while continuing to illegally receive public funds earmarked for her still born son.

Then Jezebel turned and looked directly at Mable and said, "Finally the Adversary charges this soul harboring a heart of doubt that while you were with her, that you would not keep your promise that her later days would be greater than her earlier ones." Then Jezebel stepped back to her seat, sat down and said, "The Adversary rest its case."

THE CASE FOR MABLE

Once Jezebel sat back in her seat, the woman in white stood up and began to speak, with a powerful voice she said, "My Lord, Glory to Your Name for things you have done for and with this woman. You have walked and talked with her, her whole life and she has been obedient and disobedient at times. While it is clear she had a good heart she had little control over her emotions.

The Adversary has presented her as a whore, I offer the reason for her having some many children as she is a willing vessel to nurture and love those soul's regardless of her or their circumstance, which you blessed her with. And through all the trial's and tribulations she never once rejected your love and did not offer a word about your love to someone in need of encouragement.

THE DAY AFTER LIFE

I close with this point, not as if you didn't know but to remind the Adversary that it was by your will that she was given a second chance at life and with that the desires of her heart. Who would know best her worthiness other than a merciful and loving father? I offer Mable Thomas Shelborne your servant candidate for eternal life, in your name."

Then the Lord turned to the bench, bowed low and with his hands raised high above his head he began to pray, first thanking God the Father for all He has done, then thanking Him for His Word and then making the request for the salvation of Mable Thomas Shelborne without uttering a word himself.

After a moment, that seemed to be an eternity Mable stood up, turned to look as both Jezebel and Elder Gomer stood up in anticipation of the Lord's Judgment...

THE DAY AFTER LIFE

CHAPTER 7

PASTOR WILLIE JACKSON

As the man walked away Marques said, "What was his name? You know him, from where?" Rufus smiled and said, "You know him, he's on TV every day. Whose next here, you got to get back to your post." Marques smiled and said, "Oh! You want me to go back to my post, really? Then speed this thing up, will you!"

Rufus responded and said, "You always in a hurry, what is the word you got for this Pastor?" Marques smiled and said, "You feeling me right, my anointing is on ain't it?" Rufus smiled and said, "Don't let it go to your head what is the word for him?"

Marques thought for a moment and said, "Harvest, from Leviticus the 19th chapter verses 8 through 12 the King James version '8 Therefore everyone who eats it shall bear his iniquity, because he has profaned the hallowed offering of the LORD; and that person shall be cut off from his people. 9 'When you reap the harvest of your land, you shall not wholly reap the corners of your field, nor shall you gather the gleanings of your harvest. 10 And you shall not glean your vineyard, nor shall you gather every grape of your vineyard; you shall leave them for the poor and the stranger: I am the LORD your God. 11 'You shall not steal, nor deal falsely, nor lie to one another. 12 And you shall not swear by My name falsely, nor shall you profane the name of your God: I am the LORD.'"

Then the stream began to flow and the men saw Pastor Jackson unbutton his shirt and slip a key on his gold chain next to his cross. Then he closed his shirt back up again. And then Apostle David looked back over at Lee Johnson and nodded that he was finished. Lee turned to Pastor Jackson and said, "I have one more question of you and it again only requires a simple 'Yes or No' response. You said, you know me, if you do then call my name?" Pastor Jackson looked Lee straight in the eyes and then looked at Apostle David and the young man seated next to him, then he sat back in his chair and said nothing.

After a moment Apostle David and his assistant got up and walked out as did Lee Johnson. Pastor Jackson watched the men leave the conference table, walk towards what seemed like a blank wall and then out of nowhere two separate doors appeared and then disappeared. He did note that the door that the Apostle and his aide walked through was a simple large Oak door and Mr. Lee Johnson walked through a large Birch wood door with a cut diamond handle on it. But as soon as he got up to leave the doors were no longer there nor did they reappear. ... So after standing in front of a blank wall for a few minutes Pastor Jackson decide to try exiting on the other side of the room. When he reached the far edge of the conference table he saw just beyond him an exist sign hanging over an Oak wood door. He cheerfully stepped to it and when he reached for it, it opened and he saw a beautiful gate. Through the gate he could see a great meadow with two large trees in the center with a

THE DAY AFTER LIFE

beautiful bright rainbow stretched above them.

He did not see a latch on the gate or a handle but he did notice his wife standing near one of the trees in the great meadow. His heart fluttered when he saw her and as he waved at her with one hand he reached to still his heart with the other and the gate opened. He ran toward her and when they finally embraced they were one.

THE CASE AGAINST PASTOR JACKSON

Pastor Jackson was so happy he lost all track of time, it wasn't until he suddenly realized he was no longer holding his wife and was sitting at the judgment table that he things had changed.

As he starred at the great throne that was in front of him he could not grasp the majesty of it at first. While all he could sense was love and grace he did feel an overwhelming fear in his spirit.

On his left appeared a heavy set man in a gray suit with shirt, tie and shoes to match. An outfit he had worn on may celebratory occasions at his church. The man even had a white handkerchief in his jacket pocket. Something his wife had pointed out each time he wore the same outfit. Pastor Jackson could hear her say, 'Why do you always wear a white hanky white a gray out? Why do you use the gray one that I bought you to go with that outfit?' He remembered that his response would always be the same, "I wear a white hanky because it symbolizes my surrender to the Father."

When the man to his left turned and looked at Pastor Jackson

THE DAY AFTER LIFE

he could see fire in his eyes and the spirit of death just seemed to hover over his head.

Pastor Jackson recoiled and quickly turned to his right and saw another man seated and starring at the great throne in front of them; he looked as if he was in deep thought. The man was wearing a simple white on white robe and no shoes.

For some reason Pastor Jackson's eye's drifted back to the great throne and there he saw what he thought could only be a vision of Jesus standing there at the right side of the throne looking into the heavens. He quickly bowed down and started to praise him but as he got caught up in his prayer he could hear the man on his left begin to mumble and it distracted him.

Then Jesus turned and the room filled with people, it seemed like thousands upon thousands had appeared in an instance; all quietly looking down at the four men.

Suddenly the man in the gray suit stood up and said, "Lucifer for the Prosecution, we are ready to precede, Son of God." Jesus extended his hand and nodded to proceed.

Lucifer slightly bowed and nodded then he said, "The Soul your Pastor Willie Appleton Jackson is here for final judgment. If it pleases the Father since Pastor Jackson is one of your chosen that we consider his life before that moment of acceptance to your call to serve. The Prosecution believes that while Pastor Jackson has a hedge of protection surrounding his comings and goings as your elect, that it is all a façade as he realizes the benefits of his relationship with you and finds them as the sole motivation for his obedience. The Adversary offers, had it not been for the benefits you promised him he would have not only not answered your call to serve but he would have found favor in my legend as possibly a Lead Demon or Wizard."

Jesus looked at Pastor Jackson and then back at Lucifer and nodded for him to proceed.

Lucifer looked at Pastor Jackson and grind a little smile, then he said, "I take you back to a time just weeks prior to the Soul's accepting his call to service and point to the life he had worked so hard to build: his pride, his arrogance, his lust for the life of a thug rapper.

Your Pastor Jackson was the kind of person who collected, corrupted and abused women for a living a Pimp as they call it. He had a harem of 40 women all working seven days a week 18 hour days pleasuring people for money. He sold any thing he could get his hands on; from dupe to dog food as one police man put it. He murder men, women and children just to intimidate and control the weak. He clearly was a man after my soul.

At the moment Pastor Jackson, looked over at Jesus, face to see his reaction and there was none. His reaction was as if Lucifer hadn't said anything that he didn't already know. Then Pastor Jackson looked at the man to his right and he again looked as if he was in deep thought, so he turned his attention back to Lucifer as he continued.

Then Lucifer said, "I want to remind all who will hear, this Soul

THE DAY AFTER LIFE

has said on many occasions, 'If there was a God in heaven why would he left me just blow your brains all over the street like this? (And the sound of a gun went off and echoed throughout the court room.)

Then Lucifer said, "That man woman or child he killed was sent by you; sent by you to do a work in your kingdom. If is clear that things aren't going as well as you might have planned, but I digress we are here to focus on this Soul, that of Pastor Jackson. With that I point to his activities after he answered your call to service.

No need to ask the Soul to testify whether he does or does not remember this particular instance, however that would be an expected response for the eternally condemned.

I remind this court that Pastor Jackson, even from the pulpit has fathered several children out of wedlock, which I understand is a 'No, No'.

He has continued to lie to not only his congregation but to you about his desire to give up his sinful desires such as cursing, drinking ad lusting after young girls. I submit while many of these activities never come to fruition they are in his heart of hearts."

Lucifer continued and said, "In closing I point to my opening statement, if not for your grace and mercy where would he be. If not for your hedge of protection, I say he would be right here with me." Then he sat down.

THE DAY AFTER LIFE

THE CASE FOR PASTOR JACKSON

In an instant the man to Pastor Jackson's right stood up bowed low and as he rose he said, "Glory, Glory, Glory for the things you have done, My Lord." Once he had risen he said, "I love you oh! Lord my Savior. I the Servant of the Lord Almighty a Prophet, Hosea will speak in defense of the Soul Your Pastor Willie Appleton Jackson. The Adversary has spoken many true things however in the spirit of confusion they have fallen to the ground. I present to you my spirit who has tried the Soul's by the Spirit of the Holy Ghost and him to be a true Servant of the Lord Most High. Born under a generational cursed at birth, to live a life as a wondering and permissive spirit, by a scorned Witch; until the Soul was led to his mate he knew no other way of life.

Much of his hurtful doings were the result of anger and a lack of self control. Surely the only answer or defense for the Soul's reprehensible behavior is that at the time of those sinful acts he did not know any better. Clearly once he can to you My Lord he was healed and continued to walk the life you desired of him.

Man's heart is evil because it has to learn Love so there isn't anything remotely revelatory or even unique in the Adversary's statement justifying that this Soul not being redeemed. I offer the fact that the grace and mercy you extended during his second chance at life confirms my point this Soul has repented and is truly a worthy servant of the Lord His God." Then the Prophet Hosea bowed low and took his seat again.

Then the Lord turned to the bench, bowed low and with his

THE DAY AFTER LIFE

hands raised high above his head he began to pray, first thanking God the Father for all He has done, then thanking Him for His Word and then making the request for the salvation of Pastor Willie Appleton Jackson, without uttering a word himself.

After a moment, that seemed to be an eternity Pastor Jackson stood up, turned to look as both Lucifer and The Prophet Hosea stood up in anticipation of the Lord's Judgment...

THE DAY AFTER LIFE

CHAPTER 8

MIKE ABRAHAM

… Marques paused for a moment and then he said, "Ok, ok! You won that one. Now let's see what happened to the tall scrappy kid Mike, see if you can get his story up."

By the time Rufus switched from one guest screen to the other, the Mike's story had almost finished streaming. Each of the events stream in real time and can be uploaded in real time and since Rufus' computer is only capable of logging in, in real time the men were only able to see whatever was streaming when they logged in.

Marques and Rufus opened Mike's file just in time to see Mike drop his head and say, "…That time when I was lost I promised to be a good boy if my mom would only come and get me, so when she didn't I promised that if someone would help me find my mommy that I would always be a good boy and help others. I'd forgotten about that promise over the years and now you have reminded me. So; let me say this, I will honor that promise with these funds however I am directed because it still seems as though I am still lost, and in need of help."

Then Marques said, "I hear Matthew the 18th chapter verses 32-36 of the King James Version, "32 Then his master, after he had called him, said to him, 'You wicked servant! I forgave you all that debt because you begged me. 33 Should you not also have had compassion on your fellow servant, just as I had pity on you?' 34 And his master was angry, and delivered him to the torturers until he should pay all that was due to him. 35 "So My heavenly Father also will do to you if each of you, from his heart, does not forgive his brother his trespasses."

Then Marques said to Rufus, "I think this one is going to work out good, he seems repentant, what do you think?"

Rufus looked back at Marques and said, "I see an 'S' on his chest; An 'S' for suspect." Then they both laughed.

Rufus adjusted the volume and Marques said, "Don't turn it up too loud; you want everyone to hear what we're listening too?" Rufus just smiled and turned it down slightly.

Apostle Enosh smiled and looked at Mr. Edwards then back at Mike and said, "I think you got it. Then he and his assistant got up and walked out. Once the two had left Mr. Edwards shook his head, got up and followed the men out the same way he arrived, from behind Mike's chair.

When Mike realized all of the men had left and that he did not notice a doorway coming in or going out, he became concerned. He stood up and looked around the whole room and could not determine how he or the other men had gotten in or out of the room. Then he focused on the area where the video screen had dropped down and walked over in that direction. As soon as he crossed the threshold of the far end of the conference room table, he saw an exit door sign hanging over a door that he did not see earlier.

THE DAY AFTER LIFE

When Mike reached to push the handle less door it opened and he found himself flat on his back in a hospital bed looking up at the ceiling lamps. He could hear someone say, "...doctor we have a problem, the patient is in cardiac arrest." And it seemed as though all hell broke loose. He could hear people moving, tools dropping, machines beeping and a low constant ringing sound over head. After a few minutes he heard someone say nurse clear and then he could see his body jolt upward. He didn't feel any pain though. This happened two more times and then he heard someone say, "That's it Dr. Ross you've done all you could do, he's gone now." That was when Mike thought maybe they were talking about him and he got scared and tried to speak but no one seemed to hear him. He attempted to wave his arms but couldn't, in his frustration he began to cry and that was when one of the nurses in the room noticed it and passed out. People scrabbled to catch her and revive her, and when she finally pulled herself together she said, "Dr. Ross the patient, the patient, a tear, a tear, he is crying." Mike could see the doctor turn to him and look right into his face; it was if he was looking down drain pipe for a lost ring. So Mike blinked several times as if Morris Code. He blinked a dot, dot, dot, then a dash, dash, dash, and again a dot, dot, dot. When Dr. Ross realized that Mike was using Morris Code he knew Mike was still in there, he immediately conferred with the other doctors and they started to recheck his vital signs and brain waves.

After what seemed like a life time Dr. Ross had Mike moved to another room where they propped him up so he could see better and they attempted more test to see how best to

THE DAY AFTER LIFE

communicate with him.

Finally after days of test Dr. Ross came to Mike and said, "We have done all we can do for you at this point. Until you decide to come back to us, this is pretty much how it is going to be. I've assigned my most trusted nursing team to work with you until you find your way back Mike. I pray you God speed." And he turned and walked away. Mike began to cry, and cry a lot all he could do was shed tears he couldn't holler, he couldn't whimper, he couldn't move, all he thought about was he wanted to come back but he couldn't figure out how to.

They assigned four Black nurses to him and they had to do everything for him. They had to clean him up, feed him through a straw, comb his hair and brush his teeth and turn him over every so many hours. Mike had been paralyzed from the car accident, from the neck down, but he was still alive.

Marques looked at Rufus and said, "Wow we didn't see that coming. He just went up stairs a few minutes ago." Rufus smiled and said, "Why you asking me, you wanted to see what happened to him, not me."

Then Marques said, "That's enough of that, I'm about to cry myself. That was heart breaking.' Rufus said, "To you and me, but he can't even ask them to let him go. Die I mean. He can't talk. So now what? Who won the bet?" Marques said, "What bet? You didn't say who you were betting on or what you were betting on for that matter." Rufus said, "You ain't trying to stiff me are you?" Both men laughed out loud and Marques said, "Ok! Who and what are we betting on in this one?" Rufus said,

THE DAY AFTER LIFE

"I got the winner." Marques smiled and said, "And how are you determining the winner?" Rufus said, "That's for you to determine." They both laughed out loud again and Marques said, "We'll just hold off on betting until the next group goes up, these people so far are breaking my heart." Rufus agreed and then; ...

6 months later

Everyday since the affliction mike Abrahams would wake up to his medical nightmare, looking at the white hospital room ceiling with a cold wet towel wiping the prior evenings sleep out of his eyes and the drool off of his mouth. Tears of thank you were he could respond with and all the nurses knew that.

But this morning things were very different when Mike opened his eyes he was seat at the witness table in front of the great heavenly throne. This time he opened his eyes and saw Christ standing at the right side of the throne speaking to the father. Eventhough he did not know or hear what was being said, between then he somehow knew that was what was happening.

Mike felt a cold breeze against the left side of his neck and he turned his head. Realizing that he could turn his head gave him such great joy he was about to scream with joy when he realized who was seated on his left side. It was someone he had never seen before but whom seemed very familiar for some reason. The man, tall in stature clean shaved, shoulder length jet black hair slicked back and tied in a phony tail wearing a black suit, black shirt, shoes and socks and tie. Mike starred at the man for a moment and then it came to him who he was; it was his great grandfather Jesse Abraham III. Mike had only seen one photo of him but he had heard hundreds of stories about his great business acumen and his exploits as a moonshiner in the early 1930's during the great depression.

Before Mike could speak then man stood up and said, "The Adversary is ready to proceed." Then from mike's right side he heard a voice say, "The defense is ready to proceed your Grace."

Mike turned to see who that was and when he did he saw a rather small man dressed in a long white robe. The man was so short when he sat back down his feet dangled from the chair and did not reach the floor.

The man on Mikes left began to speak and he said, "Obedience is honored while disobedience gathers consequences but the point need further clarification in that disobedience requires a repentant heart and that is the cornerstone of the Adversary's case against the Soul known as Mike Abrahams.

Mike Abrahams lived a life of disobedience and was pleased with it. Arrogance was known to be his middle name by many of his so-called friends and associates.

A cursory review of his I.H.S. form reveals a Debit or a Sin Balance. When it comes to contributing to the work of the church or to help others Mike Abrahams name will not be found.

Even when placed in an untenable situation where he was allowed to reap what he had sown, he found himself lacking the common sense to admit the truth until it was clear to him that only the truth would set him free.

When given a second chance and afflicted with a paralyzed state it was all about him and never once did he announce how grateful he was to be alive or even repent for prior sins. This Soul seems to have all the qualifications necessary to live a powerful life in the Under Heavens.

Before I close my opening remarks need I say that this Soul has never once requested salvation or forgiveness for anything that he has done; which makes him a viable candidate for serving in the Under heaven continuum." With that said, he sat back down.

By now Mike had figured out he needed to say something before things went any further but he couldn't figure out why his mouth wouldn't open. As he struggled with that the man to his right stood up and began to speak.

He said, "If it pleases the father may I comment now?" At that point Jesus Christ acknowledged him and he began to speak and said, "I am the first of many and if anyone knows what it is like to live with a grave mistake whether because of a misunderstanding or willful disobedience I do. When Eve handed me that Apple low so many years ago I knew deep in my soul that what I was about to do wasn't right. However in my mind I did not see the facts behind my impending decision. That experience should be readily applied here with the Soul Mike Abrahams.

THE DAY AFTER LIFE

The gift of salvation must be requested and as promised, it is given freely. However in this case it need be said, that a lack of knowledge must be considered. It is not clear whether the gospel on salvation was ever really explained to Mike and more importantly if it was, was he in a position to really understand what was being said.

Now with that said, Mike's second chance at life all be it under affliction my have been a bit over whelming. While clearly an artful reminder of the power of the Father and the benefits of living a godly life it may have been more than his mind would allow him to bare. So I submit that whether he is accepted into Heaven or not, his own testimony should be considerably weighted, even the more than any defense could possibly support his desire to enter heaven. My god continue to Bless us all," and with that said he sat back down in his seat.

Then the Lord turned to the great throne, bowed low and with his hands raised high above his head he began to pray, first thanking God the Father for all He has done, then thanking Him for His Word and then making the request for the salvation of the Soul Mike Abraham, without uttering a word himself.

After a moment, that seemed to be an eternity Mike stood up, turned to look as both his great grandfather Jesse Abraham and The Prophet Adam stood up in anticipation of the Lord's Judgment...

THE DAY AFTER LIFE

CHAPTER 9

THE JUDGMENT

HAROLD FRYE'S JUDGMENT:

As the men stood in anticipation of God's judgment not a sound could be heard in the vast throne room. Jesus turned to the throne and began to pray as he did throughout the proceedings and when he finished he rose to his feet and turned to the men and said, "The Father has decided, and before he speaks his command let it be known that; *God will finish what he starts if you are obedient; your dreams will come true, if you are not obedient he will not know you... His promises will not come true for you because he will not speak them into existence for your disobedience; for his word does not come back to him void,...*"

At that moment a great white cloud appeared and filled the throne room and the Angel Gabriel stepped forward from the left hand side of the throne and unrolled a proclamation, then he began to read.

"The Lord your God has heard the case for and against the Soul Harold Frye. The Lord God required one thing for the life He gave this Soul Harold Frye; that of Service.

The Soul Harold Frye lived a life of Sin and never once repented for any of it; as written in the book of Revelation (Rev. 7:14-16 NLT) [14]And I said to him, Sir, you know. And he said to me,

THE DAY AFTER LIFE

These are they which came out of great tribulation, and have washed their robes, and made them white in the blood of the Lamb. [15]Therefore are they before the throne of God, and serve him day and night in his temple: and he that sits on the throne shall dwell among them. [16]They shall hunger no more, neither thirst any more; neither shall the sun light on them, nor any heat.... "

Gabriel continued and said, "The Lord your God fines He can not sit among an unrepentant heart for there is no love for Him in said heart and the Soul Harold Frye shall reap what it has sown. Thus the Lord Your God rendered the following judgment: He does not know the Soul Harold Frye."

And with that the Soul Harold Frye disappeared from the throne room.

MABLE SHELBORNE THOMAS JUDGMENT:

Now all of the women stood in anticipation of God's judgment and not a sound could be heard in the throne room. Jesus turned to the throne and began to pray as he had done time and time again during the proceedings and when he finished he rose to his feet turned to the women and said, "The Father has decided, and before he speaks his command let it be known that; *God will finish what he starts if you are obedient; your dreams will come true, if you are not obedient he will not know you... His promises will not come true for you because he will not speak them into existence for your disobedience; for his word does not come back to him void,...*"

THE DAY AFTER LIFE

At that very moment the great cloud of God's glory filled the throne room and the Angel Michael stepped forward from the left hand side of the throne. He unrolled a proclamation, and began to read.

"The Father has heard the case for and against the Soul Mable Shelborne Thomas from whom He required one thing of the life He gave her that of 'Change'. The Lord Your God required a change in the hearts of those she came into contact with. This Soul pleased the Lord Your God by changing itself first, by having a heart for those that came across her path regardless of circumstance. The Soul loved the Lord Your God and gave the only thing it could that was of value to the Lord Your God, her time and service. It is written in the epistle to the church of Corinth (1 Cor 15:50-52 NLT) [50] Now this I say, brothers, that flesh and blood cannot inherit the kingdom of God; neither does corruption inherit incorruption. [51] Behold, I show you a mystery; We shall not all sleep, but we shall all be changed, [52] In a moment, in the twinkling of an eye, at the last trump: for the trumpet shall sound, and the dead shall be raised incorruptible, and we shall be changed. ...,"

Michael continued and said, "The Lord your God has rendered His judgment: Well Done my good and faithful servant."

And with that the Soul Mable Shelborne Thomas took a seat in the Heavenly Choir among the other saint's in the baritone section surrounding the great throne.

PASTOR WILLIE APPLETON JACKSON JUDGMENT:

THE DAY AFTER LIFE

As the men stood in anticipation of God's judgment not a sound could be heard in the throne room. Jesus turned to the throne and began to pray as he had done so many times during the proceedings and when he finished he rose to his feet and turned to the three men and said, "It is done the Father has commanded let it be known that; The Father *God will finish what he starts if you are obedient; your dreams will come true, if you are not obedient he will not know you... His promises will not come true for you because he will not speak them into existence for your disobedience; for his word does not come back to him void,..."*

Suddenly in the twinkling of an eye a great cloud of glory filled the throne room and the Angel Michael stepped forward from the left hand side of the throne. He unrolled a proclamation, and began to read.

"The Father has heard the case for and against the Soul Pastor Willie Appleton Jackson from whom He required one thing for the life He gave him; that he be a Kingdom builder. The Soul Pastor Willie Appleton Jackson answered his calling and with a repentant heart presented his body his reasonable service unto the Father to Sheppard His sheep. It is written in the book of Matthew (Matt 25:33-35 NLT) [33]And he shall set the sheep on his right hand, but the goats on the left. [34]Then shall the King say to them on his right hand, Come, you blessed of my Father, inherit the kingdom prepared for you from the foundation of the world: [35]For I was an hungered, and you gave me meat: I was thirsty, and you gave me drink: I was a stranger, and you

THE DAY AFTER LIFE

took me in: ...."

Michael continued and said, "The Lord your God has judged the Soul Pastor Willie Appleton Jackson, Well Done my good and faithful servant."

And with that the Soul Pastor Willie Appleton Jackson took a seat in the viewing gallery among the saint's in the throne room.

MIKE ABRAHAM JUDGMENT:

As the men stood in anticipation of God's judgment a peaceful quiet hovered over the throne room and not a sound could be heard. Jesus turned to the throne to pray, as he had done so many times before during the proceedings. When he finished he rose to his feet turned to the three men and said, "It is done the Father has commanded let it be known that; The Lord *God Almighty will finish what he starts if you are obedient; your dreams will come true, if you are not obedient he will not know you... His promises will not come true for you because he will not speak them into existence for your disobedience; for his word does not come back to him void,..."*

A mighty cloud of glory filled the throne room and the Angel Gabriel stepped forward from the left hand side of the throne opened a rolled up proclamation, and began to read.

"The Lord Your God has heard the case for and against the Soul Mike Abraham from whom He required one thing for the life He gave him; that he was to thirst after Him. It is written in the book of Revelations (Rev 22:1-5 NLT) [1]And he showed me a pure

THE DAY AFTER LIFE

river of water of life, clear as crystal, proceeding out of the throne of God and of the Lamb. [2]In the middle of the street of it, and on either side of the river, was there the tree of life, which bore twelve manner of fruits, and yielded her fruit every month: and the leaves of the tree were for the healing of the nations. [3]And there shall be no more curse: but the throne of God and of the Lamb shall be in it; and his servants shall serve him: [4]And they shall see his face; and his name shall be in their foreheads. [5]And there shall be no night there; and they need no candle, neither light of the sun; for the Lord God gives them light: and they shall reign for ever and ever."

Gabriel continued and said, "The Lord your God has judged the Soul Mike Abraham: Well Done my good and faithful servant." And with that the Soul Mike Abraham took a post at the gate of Heaven among the saint's to watch over the Soul's who seek to enter but have yet to ask for salvation.

THE END

THE DAY AFTER LIFE

LIST OF OTHER TITLES BY THIS AUTHOR INCLUDING
U.S. Marshal Harry Bailey, and the "The Parables of Life Series"

Title   RELEASE DATES

1- U.S. Marshal Harry Bailey and the case of the Persistent Widow
February 2013

2- U.S. Marshal Harry Bailey and the case of the Wicked Farmers
May 2013

3- U.S. Marshal Harry Bailey and the case of the Minas
September 2013

4- U.S. Marshal Harry Bailey and the case of the Hidden Treasure
December 2013

5- U.S. Marshal Harry Bailey and the case of the Friend at Midnight
March 2014

6- U.S. Marshal Harry Bailey and the case of the Foolish Virgins
June 2014

7- U.S. Marshal Harry Bailey and the case of the Good Samaritan
December 2014

8- U.S. Marshal Harry Bailey and the case of the Four Soils
May 2015

9- U.S. Marshal Harry Bailey and the case of the Lost Coin
September 2015

10-U.S. Marshal Harry Bailey and the case of the Prodigal Son
December 2015

11- U.S. Marshal Harry Bailey and the case of the Two Debtors
March 2016

12- U.S. Marshal Harry Bailey and the case of the Two Sons
September 2016

Ask about our SPECIAL EDITION of U.S. Marshal Harry Bailey and the case of the CORPORATE KILLINGS available now! www.usmarshalharrybailey.com Other titles: The Way Station, U.S. Marshal Harry Bailey and the Corporate Killings and The Game of Your Life, 2-1-1 Emergency, Clinical Trials, Criminal Mastermind, The Deadly Mailman, Beyond The Way Station, Part II—To Hell for the Holidays, and look out for the 6 volume series U.S. Marshal Harry Bailey and the "City of Prophesy" series coming in 2015.